'If the socialists wish to make socialism a definite reality, then they must recognise that the problem of social reform is fundamental and that for them there is no escape from it.'

B.R. AMBEDKAR

Annihiliation of Caste, 1936

India and Communism

B.R. Ambedkar

India and Communism

Introduction by Anand Teltumbde

LeftWord

Offset edition first published in May 2017.
Reprinted, with revised Introduction, August 2017.
Digital print edition, January 2020.

LeftWord Books
2254/2A Shadi Khampur
New Ranjit Nagar
New Delhi 110008
INDIA

LeftWord Books is the publishing division of
Naya Rasta Publishers Pvt. Ltd.

leftword.com

ISBN 978-93-80118-45-1

The text of *India and Communism* is from
Vasant Moon and Hari Narake (eds.),
Dr. Babasaheb Ambedkar: Writings and Speeches, Vol. 3,
New Delhi: Dr. Ambedkar Foundation, 2014.

CONTENTS

PUBLISHER'S NOTE

Amongst his papers, Dr. B.R. Ambedkar (1891-1956) left behind a note on a book he wished to write entitled *India and Communism*. Ambedkar had produced a table of contents for this book:

Part – I. The Pre-requisites of Communism
Chapter 1 – The Birthplace of Communism
Chapter 2 – Communism & Democracy
Chapter 3 – Communism & Social Order

Part – II. India and the Pre-requisites of Communism
Chapter 4 – The Hindu Social Order
Chapter 5 – The Basis of the Hindu Social Order
Chapter 6 – Impediments to Communism arising from the Social Order

Part – III. What Then Shall We Do?
Chapter 1 – Marx and the European Social Order
Chapter 2 – Manu and the Hindu Social Order

The only sections that he completed – or that remained in his papers – were two parts of one chapter from the second section. These two parts are from Chapter 4: The Hindu Social Order. A total of sixty-three typed pages from this book were in this folder. Nothing else remains from this outline.

In addition, and in the same file of typed material, Ambedkar had produced an outline for a book entitled *Can I be a Hindu?* This book was also not completed. One section of this book – Symbols of Hinduism – was attached to the outline. It seems to flow out of the kind of logic that he had developed in the two parts completed for *India and Communism*.

It is most likely that these pages were typed in the early 1950s.

The editorial annotations to Ambedkar's text in this volume are by the editors of *Dr. Babasaheb Ambedkar: Writings and Speeches*, Vasant Moon and Hari Narake.

Anand Teltumbde

INTRODUCTION

BRIDGING THE UNHOLY RIFT

> The only way we'll get freedom for ourselves is to identify ourselves with every oppressed people in the world.
>
> Malcolm X

To those who think Babasaheb Ambedkar (1891-1956) was against Communism or Marxism, this book should serve as another reminder that they are grossly prejudiced. He had an abiding interest in the communist movement and philosophy (Marxism), as one focused on the emancipation of the downtrodden. This is evident right from the beginning of his public life to almost his last days when he delivered a speech comparing Karl Marx with Buddha, the progenitor of the religion he had converted to barely less than two months ago. However, it is also true that he had serious reservations about accepting certain theoretical postulations of Marxism, which perhaps prevented him from taking a deeper interest in Marxism. Therefore, he remained searching for a better method (a body of thought) that would overcome the purported limitations of Marxism and still reach the end result the latter promised. Certainly, he saw that method in Buddhism.

Vested interests amongst the Dalits, however, pitched

Ambedkar firmly as the enemy of the communists. By doing this, they threw him into the camp of the reactionaries and the exploiters. They stretched this antipathy between Ambedkar and communists to such an extent that they would discard anything even remotely associated with Marxism. The fundamental category of class, through which Ambedkar viewed human society, albeit not with the same conception as Marx and Engels did, has therefore been a complete taboo for them.[1] Of late, they even refuse to accept the term *Dalit*, a quasi-class term Ambedkar used for all the Untouchable Castes. While some of them argue that after they embraced Buddhism, they are no more Dalits or that the term Dalit is too humiliating to reflect their progressed selves, some would disingenuously suggest that Ambedkar never used the term Dalit.[2] Paradoxically, they do not object to the usage of castes which Ambedkar wanted to annihilate.

This obsession of the educated middle class of Dalits against Marxism has reached farcical levels. Ambedkar had hoped that they would provide role models for the community and represent their interests in political society. But they utterly failed to meet his expectations. They are solely responsible for the paradoxical degeneration of the Dalit movement today when Ambedkar's declared enemy – Brahmanism and Capitalism – are seen as the

[1] 'The atomistic conception of individuals in a Society so greatly popularized – I was about to say vulgarized – in political orations is the greatest humbug. To say that individuals make up society is trivial; society is always composed of classes. It may be an exaggeration to assert the theory of class-conflict, but the existence of definite classes in a society is a fact.' See B.R. Ambedkar, *Castes in India: Their Mechanism, Genesis and Development*, in Vasant Moon, ed., *Dr. Babasaheb Ambedkar Writings and Speeches (BAWS)*, Vol. 1, Education Department, Govt. of Maharashtra, 1979, p. 15.

[2] Such ignorance is spread on social media by a section of the middle class Dalits. As a matter of fact, the term Dalit represents the proud legacy of struggles waged by Jotiba Phule and continued by Babasaheb Ambedkar. While Ambedkar used 'Depressed Classes', 'Untouchable Classes' in his English writings, he mostly used 'Dalit' in his Marathi speeches. See, *BAWS*, Vol. 21, that contains his Marathi speeches.

friends of Dalits, while the Marxists – identified with the world's toiling masses – become their sworn foes.

The entire post-Ambedkar Dalit movement reflects the singular obsession to treat Marxists as the enemy. This has allowed Dalit 'leaders' to remain ensconced in the ruling circles, enjoying the perks and privileges while still calling themselves Ambedkarites. Anyone who would speak of the material concerns of the Dalits would be castigated by them as communists and maligned as anti-Ambedkar. Evidence for this is visible in the very first split of the Republican Party of India (RPI), formed in 1957 – the year after Ambedkar's death. The RPI split into *durust* (correct) and *nadurust* (incorrect) factions just within a year of its formation. The B.C. Kamble faction that split the party called itself a *durust* RPI and called the rest of the party, led by Dadasaheb Gaikwad, as *nadurust* RPI. Kamble's faction argued that since Ambedkar had given the Constitution, the Dalit struggle must be conceived within the constitutional framework. Anarchic methods like *satyagrahas* or agitations were not the Ambedkarite path. He justified his separation from the Gaikwad-led RPI on grounds familiar to us today: he accused it of being under the influence of the Communists as it spoke of the material deprivation of Dalits. Gaikwad, on the other hand, saw the importance of land to the emancipation of the Dalits and wanted to launch an agitation for land redistribution.

Both Kamble and Gaikwad took support from Ambedkar's statements. Kamble used Ambedkar's exhortation to the Dalits, made in the euphoria over the Constitution, that they should use only constitutional means to win demands and shun agitational methods.[3] Gaikwad, on the other hand, used Ambedkar's lament expressed three years later to his party workers. When the

[3] Although agitational methods are not necessarily unconstitutional, they were made out to be so by the Kamble group. The constitutional methods, therefore, were legal and representational.

Marathwada unit of the Scheduled Castes Federation (SCF) led by B.S. Waghmare visited Ambedkar in Delhi in 1953, he told them that whatever he had done had only benefitted a small section of the urban Dalits and he couldn't do much for the rural Dalits. He asked them whether they could take up struggle for land to the landless. In compliance with his advice, three land *satyagrahas* took place. The first one happened in his life time itself. It was carried out by the same SCF unit in 1953 in Marathwada under the leadership of B.S. Waghmare in which 1,700 people went to jail. The second satyagraha happened in the Khandesh-Marathwada belt in 1959 under the leadership of Gaikwad in which many communists and socialists went to jail along with the Dalits. The last one was the countrywide satyagraha that took place in 1964-65, led by Gaikwad, in which hundreds of people courted arrest every day over a month. The sheer scale of this satyagraha scared the ruling classes to their bones.

The Kamble faction was in the minority. Nonetheless, it provided the opportunist elements to defect from the RPI and to ally with the ruling camp, all the while chanting the name of Ambedkar and swearing by the interests of the Dalits.

The ruling class welcomed this development and did its utmost to accelerate the collapse of the autonomous Dalit movement. Even Dalit Panther – which had been inspired by the communist Black Panthers in the United States – split along the same lines. One faction accused the other of being communists and of deviating from Ambedkar's path, this time not the constitutional but the Buddhist path. Ambedkar, the Ambedkarite path and Ambedkarism became the rhetoric by which the opportunists justified their self-seeking conduct. This debate inside the Dalit movement enabled the ruling class parties to manipulate the Dalit universe with the help of Dalit leaders.

The Bharatiya Janata Party (BJP) has a well-known Brahmanical pedigree and it has a programme that is utterly opposed to all that Ambedkar believed. Over the past two decades, the BJP has been holding the maximum number of reserved seats in Parliament and most legislative assemblies. On the eve of the 2014 parliamentary elections, it succeeded in getting almost all the notable Dalit leaders –Ram Vilas Paswan, Udit (Ram) Raj and Ramdas Athawale – into its fold.[4] The process underscored the unsaid dictum that the Dalits may walk over to the most reactionary Brahmanical party but should not touch the Communists even with a bargepole. It is the same logic by which Prakash Ambedkar, despite being a grandson of Babasaheb, is slandered as anti-Ambedkar and even branded as a Maoist sympathiser simply because he has kept away from both the BJP and the Congress. What earned him brickbats was his attempt to form a Third Front in Maharashtra with the socialists and the communists. Dalit politicians and their hangers-on among intellectuals have raised the anti-communist dictum to an art form. They wish to broker the interests of the Dalits to the ruling classes, who would do whatever it takes to thwart the germination of a radical consciousness among the Dalit masses.

Over the years, this propaganda has transformed 'Ambedkar against Marxism' into an axiom. It has become such a fixed idea that even if Ambedkar arrived today and took up cudgels for the Dalit masses, he would be condemned as anti-Ambedkar.

AMBEDKAR AND MARX

Ambedkar's relationship with Marxism has been enigmatic. Ambedkar was never a Marxist. But he did repeatedly define himself as a socialist. Like any thinking person of his time who had been disturbed by the misery of people, Ambedkar was not

[4] Anand Teltumbde, 'Three Dalit Rams Play Hanuman to BJP', *Economic and Political Weekly*, 12 April 2014, pp. 10-11.

unimpressed by the élan of the Marxist tradition. After completing his studies at Columbia University, he rushed to England and joined the London School of Economics with an expectation that his scholarship would be extended. But when it did not happen, he had to return to India in June 1917 to join the Baroda State as per the terms of his scholarship. Despite his extraordinary qualifications and reasonably high post (he was appointed as Military Secretary to H.H. the Maharaja Gaikwad of Baroda), he faced all kinds of humiliations because of his low caste. Even the lowliest peon in his own office would hurl files onto his table so that they weren't contaminated. He would not find a roof over his head easily and when he managed to get one incognito, he would be thrown out when his caste was known. It is during such a psychological ferment that the October Revolution broke out in Russia. It was an earth-shattering event, hugely enthusing to the downtrodden of the world and equally threatening to the ruling classes everywhere. However, there is nothing to show what Ambedkar felt about it.

The first comment by Ambedkar on the Russian Revolution is in the editorial of *Bahishkrut Bharat* of 27 September 1929, more than a decade after the revolution, with the revealing title *Aadhi Kalas Mag Paya* (First Top, Then Foundation). Ambedkar reproved the communist attempts to create a revolution in India without worrying about the class-consciousness of people. It was in reaction to the long drawn strike of 1928 by communists that Ambedkar wrote:

> The communists are trying to capture the labour movement in the country. The adverse impact their previous strike created on the workers' condition has posed a serious question before the working class whether to hand over the reins of their movement to the communist leaders . . . . The main aim behind the strike is not to

improve the economic condition of workers but to train them for revolution.[5]

Ambedkar wrote that the consciousness of the majority of people was not ready for the ideal society the communists wanted to create. The main thrust of his criticism thus was on the practice of the communists, that they were ignoring certain preparatory tasks and dreaming of making a revolution in the country. In response to certain comments, he wrote another article on 15 November 1929 titled *Kranti kashala mhanatat* (What is called revolution), which commented harshly on the methods the communists adopted to bring about revolution. He wrote that the communists did not pay attention to truth-untruth, just-unjust and did not even mind unleashing atrocities in pursuing their aim of establishing a state like Soviet Russia. He said that these methods were not acceptable to him because not only did they come in the way of progress of the country but they would also push it backward.[6]

The provocation for these articles came from the communist attack on Ambedkar for having cooperated with the Simon Commission against the nationalists' decision to boycott it. It also came in response to the harsh criticism for his advising Dalits to break the strike in 1929. This strike, coming close on the heels of the earlier six month-long 1928 strike, was seen by him as a reckless move by the communists, oblivious of the plight of workers, for political gains.[7] Ambedkar was not alone in his criticism of the 1929 strike nor consequential. The rival union Bombay Textile Labour Union also was against it and had advised the Muslim workers to break the strike, replacing the Marathi workers under

[5] *Bahishkrut Bharat ani Mooknayak*, Maharashtra Government, Mumbai, 2008, p. 324 (4).

[6] Ibid, p. 337 (7).

[7] G. Lieten, 'Strikers and Strike-Breakers: Bombay Textile Mills Strike, 1929', *Economic & Political Weekly*, Vol. 17, No. 14/16, 1982.

the spell of Girni Kamgar Union. However, Ambedkar was singled out as the strike breaker by both the communists and nationalists.

As we will see later, the communists were unduly sanguine about the revolutionary prospects in the country. Some of the leading lights of the communist movement had convinced themselves that India was already a mature capitalist country and therefore ripe for bringing about a revolution in the classical Marxist fashion. For instance, M.N. Roy's *India in Transition* (1922), the first Marxist study in the world of the changes in a colonial landscape under imperialist subjugation, went further in dogmatically asserting that India, like European societies, crossed the feudal stage not 'as a result of a violent revolution but as a consequence of a long-standing contact with the political and economic measures of a highly developed capitalist state'.[8] With feudalism gone, caste, which was supposed to be its feature lying in the super-structure, naturally became a rootless phenomenon of little significance in Roy's scheme. Therefore, Ambedkar's comment about constructing the superstructure before the foundation could not be called amiss. However, his use of a moral scale for judging the Marxist methods smacks of his liberal obsession and lack of appreciation for the alternate epistemology of Marxism. This early theme of ignoring the preparation of people for revolution, *a la* eradicating caste to germinate class-consciousness and the moral infirmities of communist methods, would manifest itself variously in his arguments until his death. And the theme was mostly related to the practice of the early communists and not the theory of communism, i.e., Marxism.

Ambedkar's very first published essay, *Castes in India: Their Mechanism and Genesis*, which he had presented in Professor Alexander Goldenweiser's Anthropology Seminar at Columbia

[8] M.N. Roy, *India in Transition*, Preface to the German Edition, Excerpts in *Documents*, 1917, p. 192; ibid p. 364.

University (later published in *The Indian Antiquary* in May 1917), reflects his class orientation, which may be linked to the influence of some rudimentary readings of Marxism. This class orientation remained with Ambedkar although he dealt with caste. He always used class or '*varg*' in Marathi while referring to caste. Although under the heavy influence of liberalism, which takes the individual as its pivot, young Ambedkar defies it and says that society is always composed of classes. His passage runs as follows:

> The atomistic conception of individuals in a Society so greatly popularized – I was about to say vulgarized – in political orations is the greatest humbug. To say that individuals make up society is trivial; society is always composed of classes. It may be an exaggeration to assert the theory of class-conflict, but the existence of definite classes in a society is a fact. Their basis may differ. They may be economic or intellectual or social, but an individual in a society is always a member of a class. This is a universal fact and early Hindu society could not have been an exception to this rule, and, as a matter of fact, we know it was not. If we bear this generalization in mind, our study of the genesis of caste would be very much facilitated, for we have only to determine what was the class that first made itself into a caste, for class and caste, so to say, are next door neighbours, and it is only a span that separates the two. *A Caste is an Enclosed Class.* [Emphasis mine.][9]

When he plunged into public life to fight against caste oppression of the Dalits, he did not have much to refer to by way of theory or strategy. Except for Jotiba Phule (1827-1890), whom he considered as one of his three gurus, there was a complete void so far as the struggle against Brahmanism in his times went.

[9] B.R. Ambedkar, *Castes in India*, in *BAWS*, vol. 1, Education Department, Government of Maharashtra, Mumbai, 2014, p. 15.

Phule exposed the caste system as the intrigues of Brahman-Bhatjis and targeted them along with Shetjis, moneylenders, as the tormentors of the shudra-atishudras (Backward castes and Dalits). He diagnosed that their lack of education (vidya) was the cause of their plight. Since the doors of educations were shut on them by Brahmans, he took it upon himself to start schools for them, emphasising the education of girls. Although he fought against Brahmanism, Phule did not identify it with Brahmans as some of his close associates in his movement, Sadashiv Ballal Govande, Moro Vithal Valvekar and Sakharam Paranjape, belonged to the Brahman caste. They gave him all kinds of assistance, including financial help, to run his schools for girls, when their own caste-men were furiously opposed to it.[10] Phule considered British colonial rule as a boon for the lower castes. Since sustenance of this vile system was seen being sourced from the Hindu religion, it needed to be replaced by some other religion, which he himself started in the form of *Sarvajanik Satya Dharma*. All these analyses and strategies would have an echo in Ambedkar's struggle after Phule had gone.

Beyond Phule – who died the year before Ambedkar was born – Ambedkar did not find any theory which could guide him in his battle against caste. Karl Marx (1818-1883), a contemporary of Phule, was certainly the first thinker to draw sharp attention to the highly deleterious impact of caste on Indian society and its causal link with the relations of production. In his famous essay on *The Future Results of British Rule in India* (1853) Marx characterized the Indian castes as 'the most decisive impediment to India's progress and power'.[11] Marx correctly argued that the caste system of India was based on the hereditary division of labour,

[10] Tarkateertha Laxmanshastri Joshi, *Jotirao Phule*, http://www.arvindgupta toys.com/arvindgupta/phule.pdf. Accessed: 20 September 2016.

[11] Karl Marx, 'The British Rule in India', first published in *New York Daily Tribune*, 25 June 1853.

which was inseparably linked to the unchanging technological base and subsistence economy of the Indian village community. At that time he believed that British rule would undermine the economic and technological foundations of these primitive, self-sufficient, stagnant, and isolated village communities, particularly through the spread of railways. The industrialisation and growth of commerce, facilitated by the spread of railways, would lead to the breakdown of the traditional village communities, and with them also the caste system.[12] Marx realised later that he had exaggerated the possible impact of the spread of railways on the traditional relations of production characterized by the Indian village community.[13] The important point, however, is that Marx clearly and causally connected the archaic social formation of castes in India with the relations of production. It followed logically that the abolition of the caste hierarchy and the oppression and exploitation of the 'lower' castes could not be separated from the Marxian form of class struggle.

There is no evidence that Ambedkar had ever read these essays by Marx because he does not refer to these foundational ideas about caste when he discusses the work of Marx. But the essence of this diagnosis and the prescription that followed from it – that the struggle against caste is integral with the class struggle – is never rejected by Ambedkar. Actually, he did not differentiate them and termed his struggle against caste as the class struggle itself. His only argument was that the conception of classes by the early communists, only seen for its 'economic' basis excluding social and religious oppression, was wrong. Ambedkar's articulation, however, has not been dialectical when he insists upon the priority of social and religious over economic and political. For instance,

[12] Karl Marx, 'Future Results of British Rule in India', first published in *New York Daily Tribune*, 8 August 1853.

[13] Karl Marx, *Capital*, vol. III, ch. 20.

Ambedkar makes his bigger argument that political revolutions were always preceded by religio-social revolutions. He wrote:

> Generally speaking History bears out the proposition that political revolutions have always been preceded by social and religious revolutions. The religious Reformation started by Luther was the precursor of the political emancipation of the European people. In England Puritanism led to the establishment of political liberty. Puritanism founded the new world. It was Puritanism which won the war of American Independence and Puritanism was a religious movement. The same is true of the Muslim Empire. Before the Arabs became a political power they had undergone a thorough religious revolution started by the Prophet Mohammad. Even Indian History supports the same conclusion. The political revolution led by Chandragupta was preceded by the religious and social revolution of Buddha. The political revolution led by Shivaji was preceded by the religious and social reform brought about by the saints of Maharashtra. The political revolution of the Sikhs was preceded by the religious and social revolution led by Guru Nanak.It is unnecessary to add more illustrations. These will suffice to show that the emancipation of the mind and the soul is a necessary preliminary for the political expansion of the people.[14]

When Marx wrote about caste being 'the most decisive impediment to India's progress and power' which would be weakened by the spread of capitalist industry following the introduction of railways, he did not mean that it would happen automatically without the intervention of human agency. He did not go beyond this broad observation and certainly did not say that anti-caste struggles of the victims of caste would be useless. Marx's observation about industry undermining caste

[14] *BAWS*, Vol. 1, *Annihilation of Caste*, pp. 43-44.

has seemingly failed in India, since castes are still alive with their menacing prowess. This, of course, has been celebrated as the failure of Marxism by anti-Marxists. They say that it is not merely the advent of railways (now the third largest network in the world), but also the growth of India into a major industrialised power that has failed to dent caste. Caste for them was eternal. Neither the anti-Marxists nor the early Indian Marxists were correct in their assumption about Marx's insight. The anti-Marxists and anti-communists were strong in attributing an automatic impulse to the motor of capitalism – as if capitalism itself would undermine caste hierarchy. The early Indian Marxists were wrong in undermining the importance of 'superstructural' struggles. They raised the 'base and superstructure' metaphor to a grand principle of their theory. Marx, I argue, has been proven right. The spread of capitalism, catalysed by railway infrastructure in the country, has dented caste significantly in terms of the weakening of its ritual aspects among those who were interfaced with these developments. The urban upper caste communities that constituted nodes of the supply chain tended to remove ritualistic barriers from among them to reduce their transaction costs. Castes among these communities has been reduced to mere cultural residue of the past. The very fact that castes still survive indicates the failure of those who ignored the necessity of integrating struggles against socio-cultural oppression of the caste system and economic exploitation that seamlessly manifest through it to combine with the capitalist processes.

It is not important to see whether Marx was proved right or wrong; it is important to note, however, that castes have not only survived despite the spread of capitalism in India but also have become more menacing than ever before. The causal analysis of this paradoxical development will have little to do with Marx as compared to the so-called Marxists, and much more to do with the political dynamics that played out before and after the transfer of power wherein Dalits played a part, howsoever small.

TRYST WITH CLASS

It is unfortunate that Ambedkarites have vehemently rejected class politics in their antipathy to Marxism. They need to be reminded that Babasaheb Ambedkar interpreted castes essentially in class terms – *A Caste is an Enclosed Class* – and also formulated his struggle by taking them as a class, a class of all untouchable castes, Depressed Classes or Dalit *varg* in Marathi. It is a different matter that his conception of class was not Marxian. Actually, it oscillated more towards the Weberian end rather than towards Marxian on a continuum. Nevertheless, it remained necessarily class.

During the parleys for the Morely-Minto reforms in 1909, the Muslim League had raised a dispute that the Adivasis and the untouchables were not Hindus and hence should be excluded in determining the relative share of representations to the Congress (assumed to be representative of the Hindus) and the Muslim League.[15] This provided a strong enough lever for Ambedkar to make the caste Hindus behave. At the beginning and even during the Mahad struggle (1927) he was hopeful that the advanced elements in the Hindus would come forward to undertake reforms in the Hindu society so as to alleviate the injustice done to Dalits. But all his hopes were belied by the negative responses from the caste Hindus. Immediately after Mahad, Ambedkar began issuing threats that Dalits would convert to some other religion. Once he clearly exhorted Dalits to become Musalmans and in response got some Dalits of Jalgaon (Berar) to comply with it.[16] Although he did not explicate his rationale, it would not be difficult to discern it in circumstantial terms. It reflected a dual objective: pressuring the

[15] Anand Teltumbde, *Dalits: Past, Present and Future*, Routledge, London, 2017, p. 72.

[16] *Jalgaonche (Warhad) Mahar Musalman Jhale* (Mahars of Jalgaon (Berar) became Muslims. *Bahishkrut Bharat ani Mooknayak*, p. 290 (6).

Hindus to concede to demands of the Dalits and staking claim for a share in political power. He would use this lever while successfully establishing a separate political identity of Dalits.

His moment came at the Round Table Conferences of 1930-32 organised by the British Government to discuss constitutional reforms in India. Ambedkar came into serious contention with Mahatma Gandhi and came out victorious, winning a separate political identity for Dalits. The Communal Award of the British Prime Minister Ramsay MacDonald, announced on 4 August 1932, granted separate electorates to the Untouchables along with the Forward Castes, Lower Castes, Muslims, Buddhists, Sikhs, Indian Christians, Anglo-Indians, and Europeans. Gandhi, making an exception of Dalits, did not accept it and went on a fast unto death in protest. The CPI rejected the scheme of separate electorates. The 18 communists accused in their joint statement before the additional sessions judge, Meerut, condemned both the movement of the depressed classes and the government saying, 'The government is far more interested in the mainly artificial and ultimately reactionary "depressed classes" movement and in giving them a separate electorate . . .'[17] Gandhi effectively blackmailed Ambedkar into signing what came to be known as the Poona Pact. This pact was incorporated into the Government of India Act of 1935. The Poona Pact replaced separate electorates for Dalits with the increased number of reserved seats in joint electorates and with the Congress undertaking to work for the upliftment of Dalits. The India Act 1935 promulgated to devolve power to Indians, declared general elections in 1937 for the provincial assemblies. Ambedkar founded a political party, Independent Labour Party (ILP) in August 1936, to fight these elections. It reflected his strategy to expand his constituency beyond the Untouchables, which was

[17] Raghunath Shivaram Nimbkar, *Communists Challenge Imperialism from the Dock*, National Book Agency, Calcutta, 1987, p. 249.

rather confined to his own caste Mahar. The ILP was modelled after the ideas of the Fabians – borrowing the name from the Fabian's party – the Independent Labour Party – that was founded in Britain in 1893. The British Fabian party folded into the Labour Party in 1906, after the latter had been created by the trade unions and socialist parties. The British ILP left the Labour Party in 1932. Although ILP was informed by the electoral logic, ideologically, it was closer to Ambedkar's disposition and programmatically closer to that of communists, who at that time were operating under the umbrella of the Congress as a Socialist bloc.[18]

Ambedkar had termed the ILP as a workers' party. In an interview to the *Times of India*, published on the day he formed the party (15 August 1936), he explained the name of the party, saying that the word 'Labour' was used instead of the words 'Depressed Classes' because labour included Depressed Classes as well. It only explicated his strategy to extend his appeal beyond the Depressed Classes for the ensuing elections. The manifesto of the party indeed featured them as workers; the word 'caste' occurring only once in relation to its last objective in a passing manner, 'The party will also endeavour to prevent the administration from becoming the monopoly of any single caste or community'. The party manifesto stated that in the rural sector, population pressure and fragmentation of land holdings were the main causes of poverty and proposed the solution of industrialisation so as to maintain inputs to agriculture at an optimum level and generate

[18] After the release of its leaders in the Meerut Conspiracy Case, the CPI reorganised in 1933 and was admitted into the Communist International (Comintern) in 1934. The same year leftwing elements in the Congress formed the Congress Socialist Party, which was branded by the CPI as Social Fascist. See Murari Mohan Saha (ed.), *Documents of the Revolutionary Socialist Party: Volume One 1938–1947*, Lokayata Chetana Bikash Society, Agartala, 2001, pp. 21-25. However, with the change of policy of the Comintern toward Popular Front politics, the Indian communists changed their attitude towards the Congress and the Congress Socialist Party.

the requisite surplus for investment. It advocated an extensive programme of technical education for improving efficiency and productivity and favoured the principle of state management and state ownership wherever necessary. For industrial workers and their rights, it favoured legislation to control the employment, dismissal and promotion of employees, to fix maximum hours of work, to provide for remunerative wages, leave with pay and also inexpensive and sanitary dwellings. The manifesto also proposed village level planning for housing and sanitation for modernising the outlook of the villages.

Ambedkar took up the cause of tenants (from both the Untouchable Mahars and the caste Hindu Kunbis) in the Konkan region of Maharashtra. With the support of the Congress Socialist Party, the ILP organized a huge march of 20,000 peasants in Mumbai in January 1938, the largest pre-independence peasant mobilisation in the region. It was a practical demonstration of how both 'class' and caste could be merged into a struggle.[19] As many scholars noted, Ambedkar's speech at this occasion was laden with Marxist overtones:[20]

> Really seen there are only two castes in the world – the first, that of the rich, and the second that of poor [. . .] Just as we have organised and come here today, so we must forget caste differences and religious differences to make our organisation strong.

For the attention of his 'Communist friends', he added that in spite of his reservations about Marxist theories, 'in regard to the

[19] I use 'class' in the conventional sense, reflecting only its economic dimension, though I do not accept it. I would rather insist that class in India should necessarily embed caste.

[20] Christophe Jaffrelot, *Dr Ambedkar and Untouchability: Analysing and Fighting Caste*, Hurst and Co., London, 2005, p. 76. Also Gail Omvedt, *Dalits and Democratic Revolution*, Sage, Delhi, 1994, pp. 197-89.

toilers' class struggle, I feel the Communist philosophy to be closer to us.'[21]

Ambedkar went on addressing peasant conferences all over Maharashtra and even in Gujarat. In 1938, the Bombay government (the Congress ministry) introduced the Industrial Dispute Bill in the provincial assembly with the intention of banning strikes. It was even more stringent than the Trade Disputes Act of 1929. That draconian Bill furnished a common ground for the Marxists working in the All-India Trade Union Congress (AITUC) and the Independent Labour Party led by Ambedkar to come together to have a massive strike of 100,000 workers.[22] Ambedkar took the lead in condemning the bill in the assembly and argued that the right to strike was 'simply another name for the right to freedom'.

Nothing of this however would impress the communists. The ILP was not supported and welcomed by them because they thought the struggle led by the party and Ambedkar would lead to the fragmentation of the labour vote. Ambedkar countered that the Communist leaders were fighting for the rights of the workers but never for the human rights of the scheduled caste workers. The rift, instead of closing up, began widening when Ambedkar took up class struggle.

Indeed, during the 1930s Ambedkar was at his radical best. It prompted many scholars to see him as being closest to the Marxist position. A similar illusion was created when he wrote *States and Minorities* in 1946 on behalf of the Scheduled Castes Federation (SCF), to be submitted to the Constituent Assembly (CA) as the draft for the constitution. Ambedkar wrote this text because he anticipated that he would not get into the Constituent Assembly. The SCF had just two elected seats in the 1946 elections which

[21] Jaffrelot, *Dr Ambedkar and Untouchability*, p. 198.

[22] Sukomal Sen, *Working Class of India*, Kolkata: K.P. Bagchi & Co., 1997, pp. 366-367.

were not enough to elect him to the Constituent Assembly, and no other party pledged to support his bid to win a seat there. The model Ambedkar proposed in *State and Minorities* was the model of state socialism for India. The salient elements of the model were:

> The key industries shall be owned and run by the state; the industries which are not key industries but which are basic industries shall also be owned by the state and run by the state or by corporation established by the state; the insurance shall be the a monopoly of the state and that the state shall compel every adult citizen to take out a life insurance policy commensurate with his wages; the agriculture shall be the state industry; the state shall acquire the subsisting rights in industries, insurance and agriculture land held by private individuals whether as owners, tenants or mortgages and pay them compensation in the form of debentures equal to the value, which shall be transferable and inheritable property and earn interest but which shall be redeemed as decided by the state. The nationalized lands were to be parceled out in cultivable holdings to the village cooperatives which would be supplied with requisite capital, implements, technology, and other inputs by the state in exchange of the part of the output they produced. It provided for the private property in the form of small scale and cottage industries, personal saving, domestic animals, etc.[23]

In the 1930s, Ambedkar, despite his ideological reservations, clearly appears to be extending a hand of friendship to the Communists, but the latter do not seem to be responding positively. Rather, they dogmatically kept themselves away from his struggle, considering it merely superstructural, and even called it 'reactionary', propped up by imperialism.

Ambedkar's 'radical' phase ended with the dissolution of the

[23] B.R. Ambedkar, *States and Minorities* in *BAWS*, pp. 381.

ILP and the formation of the All India Scheduled Caste Federation in 1942. At the same time he was inducted into the viceroy's executive council as a labour member. While it served the British interests in puncturing the Civil Disobedience Movement launched by the Congress, Ambedkar perhaps saw no point in pursuing class politics when the entire political domain had turned communal. Nonetheless, he became instrumental in making many laws in the interests of the working class. The British had already agreed to a transfer of power provided a Constitution was created with the consent of all parties. With the ILP strategy, he might not have a voice which could be mustered up for Dalit representation. The tenure of the SCF, however, remained unimpressive in electoral terms.

AMBEDKAR AND COMMUNISTS

The formation of the ILP, a working class party, created an impression that Ambedkar was close to Marxism during this phase and discarded it later based on his anti-communist statements. A serious Ambedkar scholar, Gail Omvedt, reflects this view when she wrote that Ambedkar was closest to the Marxist position during the 1930s but by mid 1950s he broke with 'Marxist economics' and became a 'social democrat'.[24]As a matter of fact, Ambedkar was never close to a Marxist position and had never accepted Marxist economics. However, in the same breath, it can be certainly said that he was always interested in communism and that that interest had never waned. His deep religious upbringing and intellectual grounding in liberalism and the influences of Fabianism and pragmatism during his studentship in Columbia and London School of Economics (founded by the Fabian Society

[24] Gail Omvedt, *Ambedkar Towards an Enlightened India*, New Delhi: Penguin Books, 2008.

of Great Britain) thwarted his interest in Marxism itself. Ambedkar was deeply impressed by his professor at Columbia, John Dewey. Dewey was one of the most influential American thinkers of his time. A leading Pragmatist philosopher and a Fabian socialist, Dewey was the chairman of the League for Industrial Democracy, the American counterpart of the Fabian Society of Great Britain. In fact, most of Ambedkar's objections against Marxism could be traced to Fabian tracts.[25] Similarly, 'state socialism' in *States and Minorities* also does not mean that he had accepted Marxist economics. If he had not accepted it, then the question of discarding it also does not arise.

Even a primer on Marxism will explain that mere socialism cannot be equated with Marxism. There are a variety of socialisms ranging from ancient socialism in the Old Testament or Plato's Republic down to utopian socialism, Fabian socialism, syndicalist socialism, guild socialism, democratic socialism, Gandhian socialism, state socialism and not to discount *vedic* socialism (communism) as some of our Indian comrades proposed.[26] Marx differentiated his socialism from all these versions calling it Scientific Socialism. State socialism or collective socialism arose as a reaction against the extreme individualism of the nineteenth century. Its principles are found in the works of Eduard Bernstein in Germany, Jean Juarez in France, Karl Branting in Sweden, Edward Anseelein in Belgium and received a fillip in the era of welfare state capitalism (influenced by the economic theories of John Maynard Keynes). State Socialism does not want to abolish the state but stands for removing the evils of capitalist discrimination and inequality. It stands for the idea of a welfare state. It believes that the state alone can remove exploitation and promote general welfare.

[25] Available at http://digital.library.lse.ac.uk/collections/fabiansociety. [Last accessed: 29 November 2016]

[26] For instance, S.A. Dange, *India from Primitive Communism to Slavery*, New Delhi: People's Publishing House, 1955.

It typically envisages the means of production being nationalised, the workers being given equal pay for equal work, and the state taking social justice measures in favour of weaker sections.

Historian Gail Omvedt refers to a speech by Ambedkar on 26 August 1954, criticising the government for its pro-Russian stance in foreign policy, wherein he had said that communism was 'like forest fire! It goes on burning and consuming anything and everything that comes in its way'. No one would dispute that Ambedkar was not well-disposed towards Russia or China. However, was this sentiment because of Ambedkar's opposition to Nehru, who created a false impression of friendliness towards both countries, or was it attributable to his anathema for Marxism and abhorrence of the practice of communism? This remains an open question. Moreover, barring the initial Lenin years, Soviet Russia (USSR) rather lost its sheen and depressed many of its well-wishers. As a matter of fact, it can be observed that until the 1930s, Ambedkar was not hostile towards communism; it is his experience with the Bombay communists that made him bitter about everything communist. One can find, however, that he had a tacit admiration for post-revolution Russia. Interestingly, when Joseph Stalin came to power in Russia in 1922, Ambedkar had become emotional about a communist regime that could accept a son of a poor shoemaker to be the head of the state. Notwithstanding the negative stories of terror of Stalin against his opponents that poured out from Russia, Ambedkar maintained a soft corner for Stalin. The day Stalin passed away, it is said, Ambedkar had observed a fast to condole his death.[27] His bitterness with the communists was more of a local rather than international origin and was due more to practice than theory.

[27] S.K. Biswas, *Nine Decades of Marxism in the Land of Brahminism*, Calicut: Other Books, 2008, p. 37. Biswas further claims that Ambedkar had independently tried to establish contact with Stalin and the process had an reached advanced stage. He does not cite any source for this information.

After the 1940s, Ambedkar had started making persistent anti-communist statements, which mostly had a political context. As the communists viewed Ambedkar as fragmenting their constituency, Ambedkar was equally worried about the potential attraction of communism to Dalits. After all, their constituencies hopelessly overlapped each other. On the eve of the 1946 elections, he declared through his paper, *Janata,* to 'Beware of the Communists'.[28] This bitterness grew in reciprocation. In the 1952 election, it is said that Dange had exhorted the people to void their votes but not to cast them in favour of Ambedkar. As such, the statement cited above as an indication of his discord with Marxist economics is not the first such. In the previous year in an interview given to an American Journalist Selig S. Harrison on 21 and 28 February and 9 October 1953 on the topic of weaknesses of the Communists in the state of Maharashtra, his bitterness for the communists was obvious:

> The Communist Party was originally in the hands of some Brahmin boys – Dange and others. They have been trying to win over the Maratha community and the Scheduled Castes. But they have made no headway in Maharashtra. Why? Because they are mostly a bunch of Brahmin boys. The Russians made a great mistake to entrust the Communist movement in India to them. Either the Russians didn't want Communism in India – they wanted only drummer boys – or they didn't understand.[29]

Years before that, while presiding over a District Conference of the Depressed Classes at Masur in September 1937, again an election year, Ambedkar had declared that he was a confirmed enemy of the Communists who exploited the labourers for their

[28] *Janata*, 8 and 22 December 1945, *BAWS*, Vol. 21, p. 230.

[29] *Janata*, Vol. 21, Part 1, p. 406.

political ends, and there was no possibility of joining them.[30] It was during the 1930s, when, as Gail Omvedt suggests, he was closest to the Marxists and just a year after the election, he would join hands with them in the historic march of 20,000 peasants against the *Khoti* system in January and a massive strike in September 1938 against the Industrial Disputes Bill! One can cite many such 'hot and cold' instances of his relationship with the communists. As these instances illustrate, his anti-communist statements mainly came out of anxiety to defend his turf in electoral politics. The major question is its attribution: whether they should be taken as his opposition to communism as a Marxian concept or to its practitioners? Certainly one can see that his annoyance was due to the practice of the Bombay communists with whom he had to contend.

Ambedkar's earliest confrontation with the communists occurred just after the 1927 Mahad struggle that had galvanized the Dalits in and around Bombay to agitate for their civil rights. In the wake of the 1928 strike, when the communist leaders of the Textile Workers Union approached Ambedkar for support, he pointed out the discrimination against Dalit workers in the mills. They had to drink water from separate pitchers and were prohibited from entering the higher paying weaving department because of their untouchability.[31] He asked them to fight to stop it. It was only when he threatened to break the strike by asking Dalit workers to resume work that the communist leaders took up the issue. Ambedkar in his testimony before the Simon Commission had stated:

[30] P. Radhakrishnan, *Perfidies of Power: India in the New Millennium*, Chennai: TR Publishers, 2005, p. 54.

[31] The workers in weaving departments had to join broken threads with their saliva. The caste Hindu workers would not accept touching the threads that were polluted with untouchable saliva.

> In the recent Bombay strike this matter was brought up permanently by me. I said to the members of the union that if they did not recognise the right of the depressed classes to work in all the departments, I would rather dissuade the depressed classes from taking part in the strike. They afterwards consented, most reluctantly, to include this as one of their demands, and when they presented this to the mill owners, the mill owners very rightly snubbed them and said that if this was an injustice, they certainly were not responsible for it.[32]

It may be said, in fairness, however, that this bitterness was not entirely one-sided. The communists were also cut up with Ambedkar on account of his cooperation with the Simon Commission. As Dhananjay Keer, Ambedkar's biographer, records, Ambedkar, encouraged by Frederick Stones, the manager of the group of E.D. Sassoon Mills, had asked Dalit workers, to the bitterness of Marxists and others, to call off the strike and resume work.[33] His argument was that the communists were resorting to strikes for their political objective without minding its adverse impact on the workers' lives.

The early communists' trivialising attitude towards the caste question came from the Marxian metaphor of base and superstructure. They took it literally and therefore never appreciated, rather often despised, the anti-caste movement led by Ambedkar. They believed that unless the economic base of the society is changed, there was no way to bring about a change in superstructural institutions like the caste system. With this doctrinaire attitude they had ridiculed such struggles as useless. Moreover, they were antagonistic towards it because it was seen

[32] Ambedkar's Statement before the Simon Commission on 23 October, 1928, Quoted in Gail Omvedt, *Dalit and the Democratic Revolution*, New Delhi: Sage India, 1994, p. 154.

[33] Dhananjay Keer, *Dr. Ambedkar: Life and Mission*, Mumbai: Popular Prakashan, 2016, pp. 120-121.

as divisive of the working classes, which was their constituency. Needless to say, they showed their misunderstanding of class as well as caste, and more so of Marxism. They saw class as a pure economic category and caste as the cultural one, associated with feudalism. They were blinded to the reality of caste as the life-world of people in the Indian subcontinent that pervaded every aspect of their lives. Likewise, they mistook Marxism as a creed, a quasi-religion, and adhered to it as they had previously to the Hindu *Dharmashastras*. Puritanical fidelity to the written word was what characterized the Brahmanic culture and it reflected in their practice *vis-à-vis* Marxism. Just because Marxist theory said that industrial workers were to be the vanguard of revolution, they only focused on the workers in metropolis, ignoring the plight of the vast majority of other workers.

UNMARXIST MARXISTS

Marxism is a broad theoretical framework comprising of analytical tools for bringing about revolution. It is not a definitive blueprint. Many of the constructs that are basic to it were not even defined by Marx and Engels, their originators. Marxists were supposed to apply the theory creatively within this broad framework taking into consideration the specificities of the situation. But Indian Marxists were too zealous to implant its categories and notions, European in origin and context, on a soil ill-suited to produce the desired results. Indian specificity was definitely characterised *inter alia* by the existence of castes which, however, were consciously marginalised from the party literature for decades. As a matter of fact, the early communists were so shorn of Indian reality that it was used against them by the colonial court. In the Kanpur Conspiracy Case (1924) even the public prosecutor vitriolically burst out, saying that the communists were anti-God, anti-country, anti-family and hence by no means akin to India.[34] While one need not take the enemy's vituperativeness at face value, least of all to draw inferences, there may not be much doubt that Marxists showed their unflinching adherence to the written word of Marx as though it was a religious dictum, a la *vedvakya*. Given their social background, one is inclined to attribute this *shabd pramanya* to their Brahmanic culture.

The early communists did not feel the need to think of classes in the Indian context and emulated them from Russia, ignoring even the exhortation of Lenin as early as in 1919. Lenin, who did not know the condition of countries in the East, had urged the communists at the Second All-Russian Congress of the Communist Organisations of the Peoples of the East to rely upon the 'general theory and practice of Communism, [but] you must adapt yourselves to specific conditions such as do not exist in the European country; you must be able to apply that theory and practice to conditions in which the bulk of the population are peasants, and in which the task is to wage a struggle against medieval survivals and not against capitalism'.[35] Even the Chinese Communist Party had advised the Indian communists to 'come forward at the head and fight consistently and to the end' even 'in the struggle against the caste system'.[36] Of all the countries, the record of Indian communists in not adapting themselves 'to specific conditions' becomes glaring in their ignorance of caste.

A class analysis of society is basic to the understanding of the concrete condition that Lenin speaks of. It provides the essential input for formulating strategies for class struggle leading to

[34] Quoted in Satyabrata Roychowdhury, *Left Movement in India*, 1917-1947, New Delhi: Minerva, 1977, p. 25.

[35] V. I. Lenin, *Collected Works*, Vol. XXX, Moscow, pp. 161-162.

[36] 'Open Letter to The Indian Communists from The Chinese Communist Party', July 1933, in Arindam Sen and Partha Ghosh (ed.), *Communist Movement in India, Historical Perspective and Important Documents*, Vol. I, (1917-1939), A CPI (ML) Liberation Presentation, 1991, pp. 576-77.

revolution. It is pertinent to see whether Indian communists of Ambedkar's era really bothered to comprehend classes as they existed in India. Although classes constitute a pivotal category in Marxism, Marx and Engels did not define them beyond their being conditioned by the relations of production or by 'the direct relationship of the owners of the conditions of production to the direct producers'.[37] Lenin, who had to translate Marxism into a practical revolution, had defined 'class' as follows,

> Classes are large groups of people differing from each other by the place they occupy in a historically determined system of social production, by their relation (in most cases fixed and formulated by law) to the means of production, by their role in the social organization of labour, and, consequently, by the dimensions of the share of social wealth of which they dispose and the mode of acquiring it. Classes are groups of people one of which can appropriate the labour of another owing to the different places they occupy in a definite system of social economy.[38]

If the early Indian communists, swearing by Lenin's leadership, had followed this definition, they would have certainly been confronted by the castes craving for accommodation within their class analysis. It would have led to the embedment of castes within classes and following that, the class struggle would have perforce embedded the anti-caste struggles. It further follows that there would not have been the necessity for Dalits to articulate their separate movement. The duality of caste and class that was uncritically used by everyone, and which has been the chief bane of radical politics in India, is born of this folly of the early communists, and arguably cost us the Indian revolution for now.

Even if they had followed the Russian Revolution in empirical

[37] *Capital* III, New Delhi: LeftWord, 2010, p. 791.

[38] Lenin 'A Great Beginning', *Collected Works*, Vol. 29, p. 421.

terms, they would have realised the importance of the role of the peasantry in it. The example of neighbouring China also was more apt to emulate. But the Indian communists had their doctrinaire approach and imagined India to be already a capitalist economy with the proletarian revolution being round the corner. These follies kept them engaged with trade unions, which were representative of a tiny class of industrial workers in urban centres, ignoring the peasantry in a predominantly agrarian country. This ignorance or avoidance of the peasantry kept them away from rural India where the real caste dynamics were being played out. It was for the first time that the communists in South India, on their own initiative took up the struggle of landless labourers and peasants in Thanjavur and thereby confronted caste dynamics in 1941 foregrounding the caste question in class struggle. Even when they did take up the issue of peasants the demands made were for the tenants and not always for the poor and landless peasants who were considered as a part of Kisans. No demand on the *Jajmani* system, the caste oppression in villages, found any place on the charter of demands. However, in the 'Action Plan' for 'Common', among very general economic and political demands, only one was made to the state for 'protection' of untouchables by legislation giving equal political and religious rights.[39] Neither Roy nor the Labour Kisan Party of Hindostan (LKPH) or Dange thought of caste as a serious factor to be tackled within India.

As observed above, the Congress had realized the importance of the Untouchables in their claim of share of power *vis-à-vis* the Muslim League and was seized of the issue of untouchability from 1916. However, the communists were blissfully unaware of it. When the Congress passed the Bardoli resolution 'To uplift the distressed classes', M.N. Roy referred to it as part of the Constructive

[39] G. Adhikari, ed., *Documents of the History of the Communist Party of India*, Vol. II, New Delhi: People's Publishing House, 1982, p. 121.

Programme,[40] but even thereafter paid scant attention to the issue. Clemens Dutt, the British Marxist, even outsmarted Roy stating, 'In spite of the vaunted spirituality of India and the mysticism which is supposed to be as such a feature of the Indian mind, the effects of economic factors seem to be more clearly demonstrable in India than even in materialistic Western Europe'.[41] It is clearly reflected even in the presidential address at the First Communist Conference delivered by M. Singaravelu, the person who unlike many was well aware of the social oppression of the Untouchables in Chennai:

> We shall now briefly deal with two other items of propaganda adopted by the Congress in the struggle for Swaraj. We shall first take the problem of untouchability and state my opinion as to our party's relationship to the problems. It should be clearly understood that from the standpoint of communism this question of untouchability is purely an economical problem. Whether this class of people are [sic] admitted in temples or tanks or streets is not a question connected with our fight for Swaraj. With the advent of Swaraj these social and religious disabilities will fall off themselves. Communists have neither caste nor creed nor religion. As Hindus, Mohammadans or Christians, they may have private views about them. The question of untouchability is essentially associated with economic dependence of the vast mass of these Indians. No sooner their economic dependence is solved, the social stigma of untouchability is bound to disappear.[42]

Singaravelu also added that entry into temples, tanks and roads would not 'raise these unfortunates in the social scale in

[40] 'Imprecor', Vol. II, No. 60, 21 July 1922, in Adhikari, *Documents*, Vol. I, pp. 497-498.

[41] Adhikari, *Documents*, Vol. II, p. 513.

[42] Adhikari, *Documents*, Vol. II, p. 651.

equal terms with their affluent brethren' and since untouchability being an 'essentially agrarian problem', without relieving them of economic dependence any 'talk of removing untouchability is basically insincere'.[43] This was precisely the CPI's outlook towards the problems of caste and untouchability. If it could influence a person like Singaravelu, who himself belonged to the fisherman community and had worked with Iyothee Thass Panditar and Periyar Ramasamy, the thinking of the other leaders, a majority of whom came from the Brahman caste, could be imagined.

The debate among the émigré Marxists of early years also shows that they were more concerned about whether to use or ignore the sentiment of nationalism for the revolutionary cause rather than about the material plight of the masses.[44] In time, they did debate many such issues but the question of how to adapt Marxism to the Indian condition was not their point of disagreement. Their doctrinaire approach convinced them that the revolution would be brought about only by the industrial working classes after which many other social evils would automatically vanish. This automatism informed by the 'base and superstructure' metaphor, as they understood it, wanted Dalits to forget their woes and wait for the revolution to occur!

METAPHORIC MADNESS

Base and superstructure is a metaphor that Marx and Engels used to stress the primacy of the material, a corollary of its core tenet of dialectical materialism. An early articulation of the base and superstructure relationship is found in Marx and Engel's critique of the idealism of contemporary German philosophy in

[43] Adhikari, *Documents*, Vol. II, p. 651.
[44] M.A. Persits, *Revolutionaries of India in Soviet Russia*, Moscow: Progress Publishers, 1973, pp. 205-206.

The German Ideology, written in the mid-1840s,

> Civil society as such only develops with the bourgeoisie; the social organisation evolving directly out of production and commerce, which in all ages forms the basis of the State and of the rest of the idealistic superstructure, has, however, always been designated by the same name. This conception of history depends on our ability to expound the real process of production, starting out from the material production of life itself, and to comprehend the form of intercourse connected with this and created by this mode of production (i.e. civil society in its various stages), as the basis of all history; and to show it in its action as State, to explain all the different theoretical products and forms of consciousness, religion, philosophy, ethics, etc. etc. and trace their origins and growth from that basis; by which means, of course, the whole thing can be depicted in its totality (and therefore, too, the reciprocal action of these various sides on one another).[45]

The metaphor came in the form of a relationship between the economic structure and the 'legal and political' superstructure in *The Preface to A Contribution to the Critique of Political Economy*, 1859, where Marx wrote,

> The general conclusion at which I arrived and which, once reached, became the guiding principle of my studies can be summarised as follows. In the social production of their existence, men inevitably enter into definite relations, which are independent of their will, namely relations of production appropriate to a given stage in the development of their material forces of production. The totality of these relations of production constitutes the economic structure of society, the real foundation, on which arises a legal and political superstructure and to which correspond definite forms of social

[45] Karl Marx, *The German Ideology*, marxists.org. Accessed: 28 June 2017.

> consciousness. The mode of production of material life conditions the general process of social, political and intellectual life. It is not the consciousness of men that determines their existence, but their social existence that determines their consciousness.[46]

Ever since then, Marxists began interpreting this statement: What is the 'base'? The economy? The forces of production? Technology? The relations of production? What is included in the superstructure? Obviously, the state, but what about ideology (and revolutionary theory)? The family? The state when it owns industry? Finally, what is the relation between the 'base' and the 'superstructure'? Does the base determine the superstructure? If so, what exactly is the nature of the determination? And does the superstructure have a degree of 'autonomy' – and if so, how can this be reconciled with talk of 'determination' (even if it is only 'determination in the last resort')?[47]

While debate ensued around answers to these questions, the likes of Karl Kautsky, whom Lenin once called Pope of Marxism, and Georgi Plekhanov, a leading Russian Marxist who influenced the mainstream after the October Revolution, held that the development of production automatically resulted in changes in the superstructure.[48] Following them, traditional Marxists interpreted 'base' to mean 'material reality' and 'superstructure' to mean something like 'social and intellectual phenomena' and interpreted Marx's argument to mean that there is a straightforward mechanical causality between the base and superstructure. It reduced Marxism to a deterministic or passive and fatalistic creed almost negating the role of human agency despite Marx's own

[46] http://csf.Colorado.EDU/psn/marx/Archive/1859-CPE/cpe0.txt.

[47] Chris Harman, 'Base and Superstructure', *International Socialism*, No. 32, Summer 1986, pp. 3-44; Chris Harman, *Marxism and History*, London: Bookmarks, 1998, pp. 7-54.

[48] Chris Harman, 'Base and Superstructure'.

historical writings – the *Class Struggles in France, The Eighteenth Brumaire of Louis Bonaparte, The Civil War in France* – which did not contain an iota of a hint of a passive, fatalistic approach to historical change. Engels, in a letter to Heinz Stakrenburg, responded to this gross misinterpretation of the phrase by certain Marxists. He wrote:

> Political, juridical, philosophical, religious, literary, artistic, etc. development is based on economic development. But these all react on one another and also upon the economic basis. It is not that the economic situation is cause, solely active, while everything else is only passive effect. There is rather interaction on the basis of economic necessity which ultimately always asserts itself.[49]

And in another letter to Joseph Bloch:

> According to the materialist conception of history, the ultimately determining element in history is the production and reproduction of real life. More than that neither Marx nor I have ever asserted. Hence if somebody twists this into saying that the economic element is the only determining one, he transforms that proposition into a meaningless abstract senseless phrase.
>
> The economic situation is the basis, but the various elements of the superstructure – political forms of the class struggle and its results, to wit: constitutions established by victorious classes after a successful battle, etc, juridical forms and even the reflexes of these actual struggles in the brains of the participants, political, juristic, philosophical theories, religious views and their further development into systems of dogmas – also exercise their influence upon the

[49] Letter of 25th January 1894 in Marx and Engels, *Correspondence*, International Publishers (1968). https://www.marxists.org/archive/marx/works/1894/letters/94_01_25.htm.

> course of the historical struggles and in many cases preponderate in determining their form . . .
>
> There is an interaction of all these elements in which, amid all the endless host of accidents, the economic element finally asserts itself as necessary.[50]

While all this happened in Europe, in India, the base and superstructure metaphor assumed a grotesque mechanistic form denying the existence of the stark reality of caste. Indian Marxists remained insulated from the later interpretation of this phrase by the 'new left' of the late 1950s and the Maoist left of the mid-1960s. Both of them had launched assaults on the crude mechanical determinist account of history. Many Marxist scholars noted the damage caused by this metaphor and dismissed its automatic and deterministic interpretation. Louis Althusser, a French Marxist philosopher, formalised in 1960s a new theoretical structure that effectively did away with all old notions of 'base', 'superstructure' and 'determination'. It held that society consisted of a number of different structures – the political, the economic, the ideological, and the linguistic – each developing at its own speed, and having an impact on the others. At any particular point in history it could be any one of them that dominated the others. It was only 'in the last instance' that the economic was 'determinant'.[51] Notwithstanding these interpretations, many among Indian Marxists even these days swear by this metaphor as profound theoretical tenet. They do not realise that it has been the root cause for the split between and divergence of the movement of the Indian proletariat and consequent dilapidation of both of its branches, viz., Marxist and Dalit. Over the years, Marxists have variously

[50] Letter of 21/22 September 1890. Also see his letters to Schmidt of 5 August 1890 and 27 October 1890, and his letter to Mehring of 14 July, 1893.

[51] Chris Harman, 'Base and Superstructure'; Norman Geras, 'Althusser's Marxism: An Account and Assessment', *New Left Review*, vol. 1/71, January-February 1972, p. 57.

realized the mistake of ignoring caste and Ambedkar, but they still lack conviction insofar as they are seen when driven deeper, obsessively clinging to this metaphor of base and superstructure.

The CPI did confront the existence of the caste factor in modern factories in 1930 but the AITUC hardly made any pronouncement in this regard. In its March 1931 pamphlet titled *The Karachi Congress and the Struggle against Imperialism*, it appealed to the working people and sincere revolutionary elements to keep away from the 'traitors of the National Congress' and urged them to struggle for demands like 'abolition of all caste, religious and national privileges and complete equality regardless of race, caste, sex or religion'.[52] But this – sadly – was largely empty rhetoric, without any backing in practice.

COMMUNISTS' MISDEMEANOR

As discussed, the CPI's attitude towards Ambedkar was largely rooted in its misconception of the 'base and superstructure', which was certainly supplemented by the caste prejudices of its upper caste leaders. It began to show up from Ambedkar's testimony before the Simon Commission in 1928. The CPI rejected the scheme of separate electorates when Ambedkar won them after fierce contention with Gandhi. Eighteen communists in their joint statement before the additional sessions judge, Meerut, condemned both the movement of the depressed classes and the government's reception of it. They expressed themselves stating, 'The government is far more interested in the mainly artificial and ultimately reactionary "depressed classes" movement and in giving them a separate electorate'.[53] Thus, they held similar positions as Gandhi's on the question of separate electorates, notwithstanding

[52] Sen and Ghosh, ed., *Communist Movement in India*, p. 481.
[53] Nimbkar, *Communists Challenge Imperialism From the Dock*, p. 249.

their repudiation of caste as against Gandhi's approval of it as part of *Varnashram Dharma*. Gandhi would say there was nothing sinful about caste, as there was about untouchability.[54] For Ambedkar, this nuanced favour of the communists was more irritating than Gandhi's orthodox opposition simply because it came from those who claimed to work for the downtrodden. The position of the CPI on separate electorates substantiated the criticism of Ambedkar made against the communists for their insincerity regarding the scheduled castes. Even the twenty-first session of the All-India Trade Union Congress held in Madras, on 21 and 22 January 1945, attended by 855 delegates, which was reported by B.T. Randive in the *People's War* had not even a single word referring to caste and the problems of the working class.[55]

Notwithstanding their great sacrifices, it is a sad fact that many communists could not lift themselves above the caste infirmity. To some extent caste itself manifested in their conduct subconsciously, in that they were not be able to decaste themselves. It was natural that the communist leadership came from the middle-class and upper-castes in India but this very fact cast an extra responsibility on them to show themselves above board with regard to the decadent feudal remains of caste. But unfortunately, the communist leadership made itself vulnerable to criticism for backing out against caste or Brahmanism. To some extent it is attributable to their doctrinaire attitude towards Marxism, their conscious ignorance of the problem as they feared that it would divide the ranks of the working classes but worst, it was also due to their inability to efface their caste consciousness of being upper-caste.

The more annoying was the fact that many individual

[54] Quoted in Bipan Chandra et. al, eds., *India's Struggle for Independence*, p. 294.

[55] *People's War*, Vol. III, No. 33, 11 February 1945.

comrades, even in leadership positions, openly lent expression to their caste pride and prejudice. It may be understandable if such expression emanated from the subconscious, as such deep-drawn ethos may not be erased suddenly. But if it came consciously and callously, it was certainly problematic. Leave aside the past, it is a commonplace experience of Dalit comrades, who join the communists, incurring the displeasure of their community, being reminded of their caste by their upper caste comrades. They are invariably adjectivised as Dalits. Interestingly, it seldom happens outside the communist circle. I have personally experienced umpteen numbers of times when my communist hosts introduce some XYZ comrade as 'our very committed and diligent Dalit comrade'. Initially, I used to retort by asking them their own caste. While some of them realised their mistake and apologised, some, to my dismay, told me their caste without a trace of embarrassment on their face. I realized, it was futile to react and stopped it thereafter. As Anand Patwardhan's documentary, *Jai Bhim Comrade*, depicted the pitiful plight of Dalit comrades: they become outcaste for both their own community, which they ideologically forsook, as well as to the comrades whom they embraced. The former castigates them as communist and the latter condemn them as Ambedkarite, a euphemism for a Dalit. If this is the state of affairs today, one can easily imagine what it would have been a hundred years ago.

Conscious or subconscious, at the level of individuals, it may still be condoned. But when it happens at the organisational level, it is seriously problematical. When Jiban Dhupi, a Dalit CPI activist was released after eleven years in jail in 1946, he was projected in the CPI central organ as 'Scheduled Caste Fighter against Social Injustice' with the subtitle, 'Dhupi's Son Who Found His Way to Communism'. Jiban Dhupi's life sketch was drawn as a fighter against caste Hindu oppression, who joined the Communist Party via the Anushilan Samiti, an anti-colonial terrorist outfit in Bengal. The party organ as such waxed eloquent praising this 'scheduled caste comrade': 'what our scheduled caste comrades represent in the life of our people, what they have fought for in the past and what they will fight for in the future, can be seen from the life sketch of Jiban Dhupi, scheduled caste communist fighter, just released after eleven years in jail'.[56] This kind of identification of a comrade by caste, who had such a history of personal sacrifices made to the cause of revolution being denied his class identity by an otherwise caste-blind outfit that swore by class, spoke volumes about the caste consciousness of the communists. Jiban Dhupi's depiction as a 'scheduled caste communist' was perhaps prompted by the electoral expediency to appeal to Dalits as the elections were round the corner. But then that made it a bigger sin than the habitual expressions about caste. If the communist party uses caste and other such primordial identities of people while mouthing revolutionary slogans, it is more hypocritical than its bourgeois counterparts.

The CPI did not even think of curbing the caste associations of its members or leaders. Comrade K.N. Joglekar, a prominent leader of the Bombay textile union, who led workers' strikes in 1924, 1925, 1927 and including the long-drawn out strike in 1928, and was an elected office bearer of the CPI for many years also remained a member of the Brahmin Sabha, a caste organisation of the Brahmans in Bombay.[57] It may sound incredible today but the CPI members were not officially debarred from joining caste organisations. It was only in 1927, after two years, that the Executive Committee of the CPI asked Joglekar to resign from the Brahmin Sabha.[58] In early 1934 the reorganised CPI, after the release of Dr. Gangadhar Adhikari and others from the Meerut Case

[56] *People's Age*, Vol. IV, No. 30, 20 January 1946, p.3.

[57] Sen and Ghosh, *Communist Movement in India*, p. 295.

[58] Sashi Joshi, 'Nehru and the Emergence of the Left Bloc, 1927-29', in Bipan Chandra, ed., *The Indian Left*, New Delhi: Vikas Publishing House, 1983, pp. 83-84.

in 1933, published the statutes of the Communist Party of India. The statutes in dealing with the question of party members and their duties stated that 'A member of the party is any person who recognises the programme of the Communist International, the Draft Platform of Action of the Communist Party and who works in one of the party organisations, obeys the decision of the Party and the Communist International and regularly pays membership dues.'[59] Interestingly enough, the statutes did not insert any conditionality debarring membership to persons simultaneously holding membership of any caste or communal organisation. Even the clause elaborating the situation of expulsion of a member from the party omitted any such reference.[60]

In the hundreds of speeches that communist members of the Workers and Peasants Party made during various strikes between 1927-29, which were presented as evidence in the Meerut Conspiracy Case, there was no effort at taking caste and religious loyalties 'as a serious obstacle to the growth of working class consciousness.'[61] It is reported that Jogelkar during the peak of the strike in 1928 demanded uncooked food as strike relief in an evocative speech, 'You know that there are some "Bhaiyas", i.e., up countrymen who do not eat food prepared by the others, and we also do not eat food prepared by the people of other castes.'[62] Another Marxist pioneer and trade union leader – Comrade Mirajkar – promised the striking workers that the city corporation was going

[59] *Statutes of the Communist Party of India* (published in the International Press Correspondence dated 11th May, 1934), in Indian Communist Party Documents, 1930-1956, Bombay: The Democratic Research Service, 1957, pp. 23-24.

[60] Ibid., p. 25.

[61] Meerut Conspitacy Case, Speeches, 1928, (M.C.C.), p, 1700,21.7.1928. Available: https://archive.org/stream/in.ernet.dli.2015.119669/2015.119669.The-Indian-Left-Critical-Appraisals_djvu.txt. Last accessed: 28 June 2017.

[62] Sashi Joshi found reference in the Meerut Conspiracy Case document, M.C.C.P. 1703, 24.7.2928.

to 'engage a Brahmin cook who would cook rice and curry' to be distributed to them.[63] It only reveals how the communist leaders could not leave the mental world of their caste. These people were stalwarts and among the founders of the communist movement in the country. Instead of putting up a brave resistance against the caste system they fumbled and even compromised with it. None other than S.A. Dange had confessed that among the pioneers of the AITUC 'many were caste minded'.[64]

While Dange could say this about other comrades, his own thoughts and conduct were imbued with caste consciousness. Before becoming a communist, Dange was immensely influenced by the philosophy of Lokmanya Tilak, who could be seen as the fountainhead of the ideas of Hindutva. But, even as the foremost leader of the communist movement, Dange could not discard those influences. Bani Deshpande writes: 'In fact in many places he has shown faith and agreement with the *Gita* and Tilak's *Gita Rahasya*'.[65] Dange tended to see his Marxism in the Vedas and the Bhagwad Gita. As a communist he would write, 'when the *Gita* records the testimony of Lord Krishna that he had created the four divisions on the basis of *guna* and *karma*, he means nothing less than these divisions being an economic necessity of production, distribution, that the castes had come into existence neither from sin or (nor) merit, neither from *Moksha* nor hell, but from the necessity of division of labour'.[66] Dange had no qualms in justifying the fact that the caste system grew out of social necessity and that the *Gita* on *Varnashram* system perfectly matched with Marx's

[63] Meerut Conspiracy Case, Speeches, 1928, (M.C.C.), p. 1770; 21.7.1928, ibid., p. 84.

[64] S.A. Dange, *Origins of the Trade Union Movement in India*, AITUC Publication, 1973, p. 62.

[65] Bani Deshpande, editorial note to 'Gandhi vs Lenin', S.A. Dange, *Selected Writings*, vol. 1, Mumbai: Lok Wangmaya Griha, 1974, p. 36.

[66] Dange 'The Geeta Supports Marx's Economic Determinism', editorial, *The Socialist*. No. 5, 2 September 1927; Dange, *Selected Writings*, vol. 1, p. 148.

theory of economic determination. Dange stood in contradiction with Marxist scholars like D.D. Kosambi and a host of liberal anti-caste thinkers, including Ambedkar, who considered Krishna's pronouncements in the *Gita* as the creator of the caste system providing ideological justification for this exploitative system.

When the non-Brahman movement in Maharashtra and Madras had picked up momentum in attacking Brahmans, Dange's editorials in his *Socialist* were suffused with a tone of condemnation of this movement. A few years later, in March 1928, a year after Ambedkar's Mahad struggle, which had created a significant stir in the Bombay-Pune belt, Dange presented a document of the Workers and Peasants Party of Bombay, expressing *inter alia* his strong resentment against the non-Brahman movement saying that it was against 'the chief political and intellectual leaders, who are Brahmans'.[67] He simply ignored the discrimination of the lower caste workers in the low-grade jobs in the factories and municipalities and never voiced the need for struggle against caste ideology from his platform. He believed that the growth of machine production would automatically level off caste distinctions. Dange's propositions, like those of many other communists, thus reduced the role of human agency in the fight against the caste system to the level of irrelevance. He suggested that 'every social reformer and liberator of the backward castes or of all castes must welcome and encourage the growth of the "machine", both in the factory and in the field'.[68] Dange would then supplement it with the communist slogan that final liberation from inequality and oppression would be possible when capitalism was abolished and socialism established.[69]

[67] 'The First Conference of the WPP of Bombay', in Adhikari, ed., *Documents of the History of the CPI*, Volume III, p. 249.

[68] S.A. Dange, *Mahatma Gandhi and History*, Communist Party Publication, October 1969, p. 27.

[69] Ibid, p. 28.

Much later, Dange got embroiled in a controversy for lending support to the Vedanta philosophy in 1975 by way of writing an introduction to a book titled *The Universe of Vedanta* authored by his son-in-law Bani Deshpande, who had joined the CPI in 1948. The book shocked even his most ardent followers. It contained many snippets of dubious wisdom that could have been mouthed by anyone in the contemporary Hindutva camp. He wrote, 'A scientific concept of space and time had not developed and would not be understood by anyone in the world for thousands of years except the Vedanta philosophers until Einstein at the dawn of the twentieth century, explained in modern science.'[70] 'Karl Marx with his own great genius and brilliant originality; once again unfurled the flag of Vedanta over the world, establishing its philosophy and theories, its dialectical laws and scientific outlook.'[71] Dange was exuberant in his praise for the book observing that 'in my opinion, [it] is quite an original contribution' in discharging the task of overcoming the feudal and colonial past.[72] In the debate that followed, Debiprasad Chattopadhyaya plainly retorted that Vedanta had been 'the favourite theme of brahmanical orthodoxy'. Chattopadhyaya continued that 'Vedanta as the orthodoxy claims is not a philosophy in the ordinary sense of the term. It is the only philosophy sanctified by scriptural authority'.[73] The CPI chairman Dange, along with Bani Deshpande, received a blistering attack from their party circle. The book was critically examined by the Central Executive Council of the CPI at a conference on 6 and 7 May 1975, which publicly rejected the formulations of the book. An uncompromising and unrepentant Dange, however, stuck to

70 Bani Deshpande, *The Universe of Vedanta*, Bombay: Indian Institute of Socialist Studies, 1974, p. 95.

71 Ibid., p. 153.

72 Ibid., Introduction, p. 2.

73 Debi Prasad Chattopadhay, 'Anti-Marxist Falsification of Indian Philosophy', *Party Life*, vol. XI, No. 6. 7 April 1975, p. 16.

his grounds, defended Deshpande's favourable view on Vedanta philosophy and preferred to be expelled by the party.[74] While this episode revealed the caste consciousness of the communist leader like Dange, it also stood testimony to the fact that a leader of his stature could be expelled by the communist party on this issue.

VOLLEY OF ABUSES

Of course, Ambedkar might not have known all these details – some date from after his death – but he couldn't have been totally ignorant of them either. His annoyance with communist practice only grew with the passage of time. The CPI's criticism of Ambedkar could have been plausible only if it had practiced what it professed. But ideologically refusing the necessity of battling caste, ignoring the conceptual basis of linking other forms of (non-economic) exploitation and continuing with unmindful practices *vis-à-vis* caste, these criticisms rang hollow. Right from his coming to prominence as the leader of the independent Dalit movement, the CPI was angry with him. Instead of befriending Ambedkar, they began attacking him as the divider of the working class, *mis-leader* of Dalit masses, opponent of the nationalist movement and a stooge of imperialists. They derided him as 'the reformist and separatist leader' who kept 'the untouchable masses away from the general democratic movement and to foster the illusion that the lot of untouchables could be improved by reliance on imperialism'.[75]

In March 1952, the CPI Central Committee adopted a special resolution on the SCF, but directed specifically against Ambedkar. It may be interesting to see some extracts from its content:

[74] S.A. Dange, 'On The Controversy Regarding The Book *The Universe of Vedanta*', ibid., pp. 12 – 15.

[75] 'Political Thesis, adopted at the Second Party Congress of the CPI', in *Documents of the History of the Communist Party of India*, edited by M.B. Rao, Vol. VII, 1948-50, New Delhi: PPH, 1976, pp. 15-16.

- The economically 'most exploited and socially the most oppressed' Scheduled Caste masses 'urge for economic betterment and social equality have been given a distorted and disruptive form by their pro-imperialist and opportunist leader, Dr. Ambedkar who has organised them on a communal, anti-caste Hindu basis in the SCF'.
- 'The party must sharply expose the policies of Ambedkar and wean the SCF masses away from his influence by boldly championing the democratic demands of the Scheduled Caste masses, by fighting caste-Hindu oppression against them and by drawing them into common mass organisations'.
- 'It would be a mistake, however, to adopt the same attitude towards all units of the SCF in all parts of the country . . . Many units of the SCF and several of its local leaders don't subscribe to the views and policies of Dr. Ambedkar. Every effort should be made to draw these units and individuals . . . to help the process of radicalisation among the Scheduled Caste masses'.

The CPI's resolution was clearly meant to drive a wedge between Ambedkar and his associates, and the lower level SCF workers. These communists have never been as arrogant and bitter against the caste system as against Ambedkar.

Ambedkar, on his part, never went against one of his close followers, R.B. More, for leaving him politically and joining the Communist Party. As More himself gratefully acknowledged, not only did their personal relationship remain intact but Ambedkar himself respectfully discussed the issues of politics with him whenever they met. However, this was not the case with the communists. They not only begrudged the independent movement of Dalits but also plotted to split the SCF. In Bombay, they seeded an outfit of Dalit youth workers, which met as the Democratic Scheduled Caste Youth Conference on 23-24 January 1949. The

CPI heaped adulation on it as 'an event of great significance in the struggle of Bombay's untouchable youth for human rights and against exploitation. It was the first conference of the working youth from the most oppressed and backward section of our people'.[76]

As a matter of fact, having begun his political career as a workers' leader, Ambedkar was amenable as a possible ally but the communists who operated under the cover of the Congress, which was a party truly representing the interests of the incipient bourgeoisie, saw him as a rival. Curiously, the CPI did not appreciate Ambedkar's tryst with class politics during the 1930s, but when he switched to apparently caste-based politics through the SCF in 1940s, the CPI woke up to its importance. The central organ of the CPI, *People's War*, gave wide coverage to the SCF and through that to the caste question in the party literature. B.T. Ranadive was entrusted by the party to write the first clear historical analysis of the role of the Indian National Congress and the Scheduled Caste Federation *vis-à-vis* the question of Scheduled Castes in India. In his ten-page analysis, Ranadive made a staid criticism of the Congress party's policies towards the untouchables. He supported the Charter of Rights placed by the Nagpur session of the Scheduled Castes Federation in 1942 and suggested that it should inscribe on its banner 'the demand for complete independence, rapid industrialization, liquidation of landlordism, etc., to really solve the problems of the untouchable masses'.[77] Despite this realization, Ranadive made a seething criticism of Ambedkar and his organisation for their failure to target British imperialism. While recognizing that '*Hindu India has oppressed them for years*

[76] 'In Bombay Untouchable Working Youth Meet in Conference, Pledge to Fight in Unity with All Toilers', *People's Age*, Vol. VII, No. 33, 13 February 1949, p.14.

[77] B.T. Ranadive 'Six Crore Untouchables: Their place in Independent India', *People's War*, Vol. III, No. 23, 3 December 1944.

and that oppression must be ended', he observed that '*this cannot happen unless the untouchables make their demands an integral part of the struggle for freedom and join other parties in securing power*' [stress in original].[78] BTR's argument that 'Rapid industrialization of the country, liquidation of landlordism and radical change in the mode of production . . . alone will give free scope to the vast mass of Untouchables to find independent means of livelihood, and lead to the abolition of untouchability'[79] obviously stands disproved by the experience of last seven decades.

It is noteworthy that while Ambedkar was harsh against the communists in his statements, he was not so when he spoke on Marxism. It is the greatest complement of a critique to place Marx and Buddha, whom he adored as his master, on the same plane, albeit for their goals. As a matter of fact, Ambedkar never questioned the communist philosophy. If at all, he praised it although he had serious reservations about its tenets. With hindsight though, one may observe that the strategies observed by both Ambedkar and the early communists had left little space for dialogue, there is no evidence to suggest that the communists really made an effort to create such a space.

The CPI continued its unremitting criticism of Ambedkar's reservation about adopting a firm stand on the question of complete independence. On their part, they never considered his argument that if the nationalists would insist on getting freedom from imperialist rule, they should also appreciate the Dalits' struggle for freedom from the shackles of Brahmanism. Even while condemning the merciless attacks on the SCF activists for their black flag protest against Gandhi when he came to occupy a PWD hut in the mixed working class area of Bombay on 31 March

[78] 'Third session of All-India Scheduled Caste Federation: No Call for National Unity, Dr. Ambedkar's Plan to Solve Communal Deadlock', *People's War*, Vol. III No. 48, 27 May 1945.

[79] Ibid.

1946, the CPI never forgot to attack Ambedkar, who they said, 'enabled the reformist and separatist leaders like Dr. Ambedkar to keep the untouchable masses away from the general democratic movement and to foster the illusion that the lot of untouchables could be improved by reliance on imperialism'.[80]

One notable event that the party immediately reacted to, at this time, was Ambedkar's resigning the post of cabinet minister at the Centre in 1951. The CPI political correspondent ridiculed his exit 'in a dramatic manner' in a bid 'to capture the imagination of the millions of Scheduled Castes as a great champion of social progress'. Ambedkar castigated the government for dropping the Hindu Code Bill and characterised it as a betrayal of the Schedule Castes. The political correspondent raked up the ugly visage of the Congress over the previous four years leading to great sufferings of the people, particularly of the 'Scheduled Castes, forming the most backward and downtrodden sections, more than anybody else'. He smelt in Ambedkar's decision an ambition to refurbish his pro-SC image after tolerating years of misrule by the Congress. In a hostile criticism, the correspondent reminded the readers that the leaders of the Federation '*Kept the Scheduled Castes out of the national movement by exploiting their just grievances against the Congress, they developed separatist tendencies among them, prevented their radicalisation and helped, along with the communal Muslim League leaders, the astute British imperialists in playing their diabolical game of divide and rule. They advanced neither the cause of India's political emancipation nor economic and social progress*' [stress in original].[81] The caption of this article – *Ambedkar's move to detach Scheduled Castes from the Left* – contained the keynote of the criticism. That Ambedkar still inspired the imagination of

[80] 'Political Thesis, adopted at the Second Party Congress of the CPI', in *Documents of the History of the Communist Party of India*, p. 111.

[81] *Cross Roads*, Vol. II, No. 24, 19 October 1951, p. 2.

the SCs more than the CPI was surely a cause of worry for the latter. The political correspondent took pains to enlighten the SCs that 'Communists Have Fought For Them' but the SCF 'decided not to enter into any election alliance with the Communist Party of India'. The CPI, he claimed, 'has consistently fought for the demands of the Scheduled Castes, it has a programme for them, it has programme for the economic reconstruction of the country, which alone can guarantee the progress of all backward sections'.

Even when they sympathised with the struggles of Dalits, the CPI never missed an opportunity to attack Ambedkar's leadership. When the SCF units in Pune and Lucknow protested against the Cabinet Mission's refusal to recognize the Dalits as a minority community, they were arrested and tortured by the police on 15 July 1946. The *People's Age* editorial, while condemning the torture and arrest, unleashed a bitter criticism of Ambedkar for his 'reliance on the British' causing immense harm to the cause of untouchables. The way to the liberation of millions of untouchables, it asserted, 'can only be achieved by the common struggle of workers and peasants against the British rulers, against the present plan and the present social system'.

QUESTION OF IMPERIALISM

Another cause (or shall I say, a pretext) for the rift between the Dalit and the communist movements is the issue of imperialism. While the communists hankered on imperialism as the main enemy and the so-called nationalist forces as their friends, Dalits saw it otherwise. Although unintended, colonial rule had brought them many benefits – the wherewithal to rise against their inhuman oppression. One can empirically see that almost all that Dalits have today in the name of safeguards were won during the colonial times. The post-colonial rulers merely adopted them under the force of the situation but not without brahmanical intrigues, which would be detrimental to their interests. Not Ambedkar alone but most Dalit leaders independent of Ambedkar held the same view about the nationalist forces. Dalits saw them as the traditional elite class/caste people, wanting to bring back their rule which meant re-enslavement of Dalits.

Ambedkar also wanted freedom from colonial rule but he insisted that the same should be guaranteed to Dalits. In his contention with the caste Hindus he saw colonial rule as the neutral arbiter. Therefore, he wanted to secure adequate institutional safeguards for Dalits before the British left India. If one looked at the conduct of the caste Hindus, including the so-called nationalists, *vis-à-vis* Dalits during those days and thereafter, one cannot fault Ambedkar for keeping away from the 'nationalist' struggle. As a democrat, Ambedkar was against imperialism but he did not think that the so-called nationalist struggle led by the Congress was really anti-imperialist. When the communists still persist in evaluation of Ambedkar on the scale of anti-imperialism, they only betray their superficial understanding of imperialism and worse, lack of empathy for Dalit issues.

The concept of imperialism entered the communist lexicon through the writings of Lenin. He saw that the competitive industrial capitalism of Marx's times had given way to finance capital (combination of industrial and bank capital), which in turn created imperialist blocks seeking to control developing countries. The ensuing competition between these imperialist blocks would result in internecine world wars, which would be the moment for the communist forces to strike at the weakest links, thus ushering into the world revolution.[82] This promise of winning the world

[82] Lenin wrote his pamphlet *Imperialism, the Highest Stage of Capitalism: A Popular Outline* synthesizing the insights of *Imperialism: A Study* (1902) by John A. Hobson, an English economist, and *Finance Capital* (*Das Finanzcapital*) (1910) by Rudolf Hilferding, an Austrian Marxist, and applying them to the new geopolitical circumstances of the First World

gripped the communists so much that thereafter this empirical observation of Lenin would nearly eclipse the theoretical discovery of Marx and Engels. They would simply forget the fundamentals of Marxism and the class struggle, the prime mover of revolutions. Arguably, Marx's theory was adequate to deal with the phenomenon. Marx in the second volume of *Capital* had explained that circuit of capital had three moments: money capital, productive capital, and merchant capital, and that anyone of them could dominate over the others. The contemporary 'supply chain' paradigm that created Walmart-like behemoths best illustrates it.

As a matter of fact, nationalism should be regarded as antithetical to communists whose ideology is primarily internationalism. The accusation against Ambedkar for ignoring the 'nationalist' struggle should thus be basically problematic. Ambedkar's notion of every caste being a nation in India better reflected the Indian reality rather than imagining India as a nation. Moreover, when Ambedkar is accused of not being anti-imperialist, one could rather find the conduct of early communists to be wanting. Initially, guided by the Comintern,[83] the communists regarded the freedom struggle as a movement of the reactionary bourgeoisie and advocated militant struggle against the capitalist and landlords. The 1929 Meerut Conspiracy case drove them underground. The British had banned communist

War, wherein capitalist imperial competition had provoked global war among the German Empire, the British Empire, the French Empire, the Tsarist Russian Empire, and their respective allies. It was thus an observation based on empirical facts.

[83] The Communist International, abbreviated as Comintern (1919–1943), also known as the Third International, was an international communist organization that advocated world communism. The International intended to fight 'by all available means, including armed force, for the overthrow of the international bourgeoisie and for the creation of an international Soviet republic as a transition stage to the complete abolition of the State'. https://www.marxists.org/history/archive/ransome/works/1919-russia/ch27.htm. Accessed: 28 June 2017.

activities from 1934 to 1938, during which they operated as part of the Congress Socialist Party. After the adoption of the Dimitrov thesis by the Comintern, which advocated for a popular front against fascism, the CPI declared support for the Congress in 1938. Many communist leaders like E.M.S. Namboodiripad, Dinkar Mehta, Sajjad Zaheer, and Soli Batliwala had become members of the national executive of the Congress Socialist Party. The CPI was again banned by the British in 1939 for its initial anti-War stance.[84] Following the Nazi-Soviet Pact of 1939, the CPI attitude towards the war – at least in its formal pronouncements – seemed to change. When Hitler attacked Poland, the CPI had called World War II an imperialist war. But when he attacked the Soviet Union, it became the People's War. Britain legalized the CPI following the rapprochement around the war and anti-fascist activities of the communists. The calls of 'Grow more Food' and 'Fight against destructive activities in factories and villages' came alongside earlier militant slogans against capitalists and landlords. In May 1943 the Central Committee exhorted members to 'Raise the united voice; we need Gandhi to end the national crisis'.[85] In view of this snapshot of history of this period, what is the point in accusing Ambedkar, who was least concerned with these issues, of not taking an anti-imperialist stand? Neither communists nor Ambedkar can be denigrated for their stand on nationalism because for both communists and Ambedkar, people were the focus and not the imagined nation. This focus on the people is what unites their horizon.

[84] The CPI had a massive general strike with participation of 92,000 workers in October 1939, the first anti-war protest in the entire international labour movement. Habib Manzer cited in Vijay Prashad, 'Introduction', *Communist Histories*, Vol. I, ed. Vijay Prashad, New Delhi: LeftWord, 2016, p. 11.

[85] 'Resolution adopted in the Central Committee meeting held on 15 February 1943', in *Communist der karmaniti, Bharater Communist Party* [Bengali], August 1942.

OPPOSING COMMUNISTS

It may be noted that the Marxists were not concerned about answering Ambedkar's complaint that they were never tired of spitting fire against imperialism but ignored the internal imperialism of the caste system. They would easily ally with the bourgeois nationalists (although Marxism professed internationalism) but oppose the organic proletariat's battle against the basic evil that thwarted this country from becoming a nation. Ambedkar on his part, it may be safely observed, was not antagonistic to the communists. The rift between the two was rather created by the communists taking an open stand against him after his meeting with the Simon Commission. It was in response to the communist criticism that he also began speaking against them.

Even then Ambedkar's opposition to communists related with their conduct and not with their creed, Marxism. As a matter of fact, in his entire discourse on Marxism or communism, he never engaged with, let alone questioned, the theoretical tenets of Marxism. In the public rally attended by over 100,000 people against the Government's move to ban strikes in 1938, Ambedkar spoke in the presence of the then stalwarts of the CPI, 'I have definitely read studiously more books on the communist philosophy than all the communist leaders here. However beautiful the communist philosophy is in those books, still it has to be seen how useful it can be made in practice. And if work is done from that perspective, I feel that the labour and length of time needed to win success in Russia will not be so much in India. And so in regard to the toilers' class struggle, I feel the Communist Philosophy to be closer to us.'[86] It did suggest that he was in agreement with or impressed by Marxism as a philosophy, but had reservations about its practicability in India. All his polemical contentions with

[86] *Janata*, 15 January 1938.

communists or communism relate with practice, not theory.

Marxism is an integral system whose core lies in dialectical materialism, which Marx discovered to be inherent in all processes in the universe. Dialectics in philosophy has been propounded by many philosophers from ancient times to a varying degree, and materialism also has been in vogue in philosophy, the typical example from India being Lokayat philosophers. Marx systemised it at the philosophical level and validated it, looking at various processes in natural science and simultaneously at the history of man. In this process, Marx derived historical materialism and saw it extending to a specific form of socialism which he termed 'scientific socialism' in order to distinguish it from various forms of socialism that were in vogue. He deduced that society will reach its ideal state that he called communism from the present phase of capitalism. With the concern for 'changing the world', he mainly focused on analysing the processes comprising contemporary capitalism and formulated his labour theory of value. He saw that while the motive force behind history has always been the contradictions between classes (class struggle), the classes in earlier phases were not as pronounced as in capitalism. For the first time in history, two main antagonistic classes emerge in capitalism, which would speed up the process of development more than even in the past. None of the components of this body has been brought into question by Ambedkar. All his comments essentially hovered around the practice of Marxism, in that, practice of the communists in his vicinity, and within the frame of liberalism.

It is only in his speech – *Buddha and Karl Marx* – that Ambedkar dwells upon Marxism away from its practice. Here too Ambedkar reveals his acceptance of its goals being the same as that of the Buddha but faults it on two counts in its methodology. They were its reliance on violence and dictatorship. Surely, going by what has happened on the ground in Marxist revolutions so far, one will be inclined to accept these observations. They are, however, not essential to Marxist theory – for Marx did not justify violence anywhere, although at places one may tend to derive that impression.

Marxism represents the greatest emancipatory project in the history of Western and even non-Western thought. No other body of ideas has so closely identified itself with the poor and the oppressed, so passionately championed their cause, devoted so much attention to a systematic study of the causes of their predicament, and dared to construct a vision of the world free from most man-made suffering.[87] The theoretical core of Marxism, dialectical materialism, states that any qualitative transformation happens when contradictions within the old system reach their uppermost limits and demands input of a chunk of energy, akin to the latent energy required in phase transition in physics. Marx called this force 'the midwife of every old society pregnant with a new one'. Many superficial critics of the communists point to this statement by Marx as indicating that the proletarian revolution will be an orgy of violence. It was Kautsky who first translated it as violence and he being the authority, a 'Pope of Marxism' as Lenin called him, was faithfully followed by subsequent Marxists. Insofar as Marx's metaphorical expression goes, anyone can see that force is not violence and a midwife is not an essential agent in the process of birth. As Daniel De Leon aptly pointed out, Marx does not sum up a revolution in terms of force. The midwife force only intervenes at the critical moment of birth. The development leading up to the birth, its time and place, are factors outside the control of the midwife.[88] Later, even Marx, appears to allude to the possibility of peaceful revolution in a country like England.

In 1872, while speaking at a public meeting in Amsterdam,

[87] Bhikhu Parekh, 'Marxism and the Problem of Violence', *Development and Change*, Vol. 23, (1992) no. 3, 103-120.

[88] W.M. Paul, 'Force: The Midwife of Revolution', https://www.marxists.org/archive/paul-william/articles/1922/force.htm. Accessed: 29 Nov. 2016.

following the Hague Congress of the First International, he declared that the means of attaining power for the working classes are not the same everywhere. He said,

> You know that the institutions, mores, and traditions of various countries must be taken into consideration, and we do not deny that there are countries – such as America, England, and if I were more familiar with your institutions, I would perhaps also add Holland – where the workers can attain their goal by peaceful means. This being the case, we must also recognize the fact that in most countries on the Continent the lever of our revolution must be force; it is force to which we must some day appeal in order to erect the rule of labour.[89]

Marx spoke of his belief in the possibility of a peaceful revolution in America, England and Holland. He took the same line in 1876 when he wrote,

> A historical development can only remain 'peaceful' so long as it is not opposed by the violence of those who wield power in society at that time. If in England or the United States, for example, the working class were to gain a majority in parliament or Congress, then it could by legal means set aside the laws and structures that stood in its way.[90]

Were the proletariat to gain a voting majority, Marx continued, any violence would come from the other side. However, in 1871, Marx blamed the Paris Commune for not being willing to start a civil war, and declared at the Congress of the International in the

[89] Speech delivered by Karl Marx on September 8, 1872, in Amsterdam; https://www.marxists.org/archive/marx/works/1872/09/08.htm. Accessed: 28 June 2017.

[90] Jack A. Goldstone, *The Encyclopedia of Political Revolutions*, New York: Routledge, 2014, p. 144.

same year, 'we must make clear to the government, we know that you are the armed power that is directed against the proletariat; we will proceed against you by peaceful means where that is possible and with arms when it is necessary'.[91] But however much both Marx and Engels may have thought that force was sometimes the midwife of revolution, they never (except briefly in 1848 and under tsarist conditions in Russia) approved of the use of revolutionary terror. They strongly criticised the use of terror by the Jacobins in the French Revolution. Its use was, for Marx and Engels, a sign of the weakness and immaturity of that revolution, which had tried to impose by sheer force what was not yet inherent in society.[92] Marx and Engels however envisaged the use of force as a revolutionary weapon if the economic, social and political conditions warranted it.

It was also Marx's view that a successful revolution – at least in the long run – was impossible if confined to one country. In the *Class Struggle in France*, Marx criticized the leaders of the French proletariat for thinking that they could consummate a proletarian revolution within France surrounded by bourgeois nations. But Marx believed equally that the degree of working-class organisation necessary to produce an international revolution could only be achieved by building up working-class parties within existing countries. Marx was strongly in favour of the unification of Germany and Italy from this internationalist perspective.

Every communist desires, most fervently, that the new social order may be established with the minimum of social friction. But desires and hopes alone do not settle historical problems. The first formulated statement of the Marxist position on the question of a peaceful revolution appears in Engels' *Principles of Communism*, written in 1847. In response to the question - 'Will it be possible to bring about the abolition of private property by

[91] N. Jayapalan, *Sociological Theory*, Delhi: Atlantic Publishers, 2001, p. 58

[92] Goldstone, *The Encyclopedia of Political Revolutions*, p. 344.

peaceful methods?' – Engels wrote, 'It is to be desired that this could happen, and communists certainly would be the last to resist it . . . But they also see that the development of the proletariat is in nearly every civilized country forcibly suppressed. Should the oppressed proletariat in the end be goaded into a revolution, we communists will then defend the cause of the proletarians by deed just as well as we do now by word.'[93]

In his *Anti Dühring*, Engels discussed this problem in some detail:

> To Herr Dühring, force is the absolute evil; the first act of force is to him the original sin; his whole exposition is a jeremiad on the contamination of all subsequent history consummated by this original sin; a jeremiad on the shameful perversion of all natural and social laws by this diabolical power, force. That force, however, plays yet another role in history, a revolutionary role; that, in the words of Marx, it is the midwife of every old society pregnant with a new one, that it is the instrument with the aid of which social movement forces its way through and shatters the dead, fossilised political forms.[94]

Violence cannot be seen in absolutist terms simply because it is integral to life. The Buddha's perspective may rather be useful to differentiate between purposeful violence and natural violence; as he advised, the former should be certainly avoided. Human history, however, is replete with purposeful violence, human lust for accumulation being its motive force. In class terms, the dominant classes always use violence to suppress the dominated masses. In capitalism, capitalists are bound to use violence to keep the working classes under control. If the latter gain consciousness

[93] Frederic Engels, *The Principles of Communism*, https://www.marxists.org/archive/marx/works/1847/11/prin-com.htm. Acccessed: 27 June 2017.

[94] Norman Geras, 'Althusser's Marxism', p. 57.

and use violence to resist it, how could it be amoral? Marx saw that the moral structure itself is relative to class composition of the society. As such, whether and when violence is to be used is a 'mere question of tactics' to be decided 'solely on the basis of utility'.[95] It may be said, that unlike bourgeois violence, proletarian violence leads to a higher stage of human development and should therefore be progressive and morally justified. While any loss of life should be summarily undesirable, in the context of revolutionary violence, Marcuse's 'calculus of progress', involving a comparative assessment of the number of people likely to be killed during and after the revolution and if the existing order were to be allowed to continue, might be a useful utility.[96] Barrington Moore's use of such an assessment to compare China favourably with India and Ted Honderich's democratic violence are more recent examples of such a consequentialist calculation.[97]As the Marxist Helmut Fleischer puts it, 'To Marxists the question [is] . . . whether the sacrifices of the revolutionary struggle and subsequent reconstruction are not less than those involved in the continuation of the status quo'.[98]Ambedkar's liberal and moral framework may detest violence but Marx's historical and species' framework would deny morality itself its autonomy, and rather defend the defensive violence of the proletariat against the violence of the ruling classes unleashed through their state. On its own, Marxism is against violence.

Ambedkar additionally faults Marxism for its lack of

[95] Eckard Bolsinger, *The Autonomy of the Political: Schmitt's and Lenin's Political Realism*, London: Greenwood Press, 2001, p. 71.

[96] Andrew Feenberg and William Leiss, eds., *The Essential Marcuse: Selected Writings of Philosopher and Social Critic*, Boston: Beacon Press, 2007, p. 49.

[97] Barrington Moore, *Social Origins of Dictatorship and Democracy*, London: Penguin, 1969 and Ted Honderich, *Terrorism for Humanity: Inquiries in Political Philosophy*, London: Pluto Press, 2003.

[98] Helmut Fleischer, *Marxism and History*, translated by Eric Mosbacher, New York: Harper & Row, 1973, p. 105.

commitment to democracy, which comes from his misreading of a phrase, 'dictatorship of the proletariat'. The expression was rarely used by Marx, and never in documents for publication, though Engels did later cite the Paris Commune as a good example of the dictatorship of the proletariat. In a letter to his friend Joseph Weydemeyer, Marx claimed as one of his contributions to socialist theory the idea that 'the class struggle necessarily leads to the dictatorship of the proletariat; that this dictatorship itself is only a transitional stage toward the abolition of all classes'. And in the *Critique of the Gotha Program* Marx wrote that when capitalist society was being transformed into communist society there would be 'a political transition period during which the state can be nothing but the revolutionary dictatorship of the proletariat'. It should be noted that the word dictatorship did not have quite the same connotation for Marx and Engels that it does for us. They associated it principally with the Roman office of *dictatura*, where all power was legally concentrated in the hands of a single man during a limited period in times of crisis.

This term 'dictatorship' is used to contrast the prevailing regime of bourgeois democracy, which in essence is the dictatorship of capitalists. There is thus a basic clash in the conceptual frameworks of Ambedkar and Marx. Ambedkar himself faulted the bourgeois parliamentary model of democracy as only the notional or political model of democracy that enshrines equal rights of all vote-worthy individuals and periodic elections to choose their representative in government. He emphatically observed that mere political democracy would be of no use unless it is supplemented by social and economic democracy. Ambedkar, therefore, defined his democracy with the expression, 'Liberty, Equality, Fraternity', claimed to have been taken from Buddhism. In the liberal framework of Ambedkar, such a paradigm as he envisaged is impossible to accomplish. He himself had a brush with this fact in the Constituent Assembly, wherein he began with an inspiring criticism of Nehru's objective resolution that the democratic republic aspiring to do social, economic and political justice was not possible without society being structured as socialist society. He said, 'I do not understand how it could be possible for any future Government which believes in doing justice socially, economically and politically, unless its economy is a socialistic economy'.[99] But he realised that he could not stretch it any further and said, 'I am however prepared to leave this subject where it is with the observations I have made'. However, while speaking about the Constitution in a euphoric moment, he did not hesitate in warning that the structure of political democracy that the Constituent Assembly created would be blasted off by the people if economic and social democracy are not brought about soonest.

Not many years later, Ambedkar would publicly disown the Constitution, saying, 'I was a hack. What I was asked to do, I did much against my will . . . But I am quite prepared to say that I shall be the first person to burn it out. I do not want it. It does not suit anybody'.[100] These words of disillusionment speaks volumes about the so-called democracy that we have. It may sound paradoxical, but if one considers Ambedkar's conception of democracy, it is not dissimilar from that of Marx. Ambedkar's democracy was 'a model of associated living. The roots of democracy are to be searched in social relationship, in terms of the associated life between the people who form the society'. By Ambedkar's own definition what we have is at the most a truncated democracy, only a third of it. The peoples' struggles all over the country are demanding nothing more than what he himself wanted the rulers to bring in at the earliest possible. But instead of realising it, the rulers use guns to suppress them.

[99] B.R. Ambedkar, 'Entry into the Constituent Assembly', in *BAWS*, vol. 13, p. 9.

[100] *Rajya Sabha,* 2 September 1953.

AMBEDKAR AND COMMUNISM

Ambedkar spoke out about his reservations on Marxism. If he had completed this book which he had called *India and Communism*. Planned towards the end of his life, it would have thrown more light on what he thought about it. Fortunately for us there are two chapters from this book to surmise the content of the balance of the chapters. Part I of the book, titled *The Pre-requisites of Communism* contained three chapters. Chapter 1 appears to be descriptive, stressing the difference between the social structures of Western Europe, especially Germany and England, associated with Marx and Engels, and that of India, where caste rules the roost. Ambedkar might have emphasized the congeniality of soil in Europe for that kind of idea – socialism – to germinate. Perhaps he might have dwelt upon the social and religious revolutions that befell those societies as referred to in his *Annihilation of Caste* and perhaps described the content of the European Renaissance and how it catalysed consciousness in people to bring about a series of revolutions. He could have contrasted it with the fossilised Indian society that could not produce any such philosophy, mainly due to the caste system. The second chapter is on communism and democracy on which his views are well known through his speech, *Buddha and Karl Marx*. The third chapter 'Communism & Social Order' perhaps might have been his view of how this communist society would look. One can also guess, what he would think of it. According to him, communism would bring equality but not liberty and fraternity as communism subordinates the individual to the collective and hence curbs individual liberty. Since only free individuals could develop a sense of fellow-feeling, it is unlikely that the communist social order would have fraternity. This is, as we have shown, Ambedkar's view, rooted in his liberal world-view.

We are fortunate to have two of three chapters from Part II of the book: Chapter 4, 'The Hindu Social Order', and chapter 5,

'The Basis of the Hindu Social Order'. Ambedkar explained how the Hindu social order was not a free social order. He gave two fundamental criteria for a free social order. The first one is that the individual is an end in himself and that the aim and object of society is the growth of the individual and the development of his personality. Society is not above an individual and if an individual has to subordinate himself to society, it is because such subordination is for his betterment and only to the extent necessary. The second essential is that the terms of associated life between members of society must be regarded by consideration founded on liberty, equality and fraternity. Chapter 6 was to discuss the impediments to communism arising from the social order. What impediments would he have listed? The foremost is of course caste and Brahmanism that informs it. He also had indicated in *Annihilation of Caste* the necessity for the destruction of the Hindu Dharmashastras, particularly the Smrutis and Puranas. Unless the larger population is freed of this garbage, he would reiterate that revolutionary class-consciousness would be unthinkable in India.

In the third section of the book, 'What then shall we do?', there are two chapters: Chapter 1 – 'Marx and the European Social Order' and Chapter 2 – 'Manu and the Hindu Social Order'. One does not know what would have been the contents of these chapters. The chapters were perhaps not written and no notes are left amongst his papers. Probably, he would have discussed the ways and means to transcend these social orders to create communist society. Or else he might have compared Marx's impact on a society where – as Marx wrote in *Capital* – the idea of equality had become 'a popular prejudice' as against a social order where – as Manu would have it – equality is anathema. India's soil needs to be made fertile for communism. It is sterile because of Manuism, the barrier to Marxism.

The importance of this incomplete book is not as much in its content as it is in the message that Ambedkar cared for communism. Despite the history of bitterness between him and the communists in India, he cared to think of reminding Indians about the prerequisites for communism. If he had been antagonistically oriented towards Marxism as propagandised by vested interests, one could logically ask why would he worry about thinking of impediments in the path of communism in India? If he had concluded that communism was trash, why would he write to Gaikwad in 1952 and 1953 that 'I am inclined to think that our people may join the communists if they think that can give them immediate relief?' All this also does not mean that he was positively disposed towards communism. All that it means is that he knew communism was certainly an emancipatory philosophy and had a huge attraction for the toiling masses, but did not have much to offer in direct terms to Dalits who were not as much the victims of economic exploitation as they were the victims of the oppressive social structure. He was absolutely right in saying that unless caste consciousness is wiped out, class-consciousness would not germinate. The only proviso I would add is that this is not a question of one or the other but a question of struggle against caste as a class. It is only through struggle that caste consciousness would be displaced and class-consciousness germinated.

The very fact that Ambedkar planned such a book, outlining the preconditions for communism, shows that he respected communism as desirable but did not see it as feasible without the accomplishment of certain other tasks. He certainly thought, as reflected in many of his writings starting from *Annihilation of Caste*, that Indian society was not yet ready for communist revolution. For instance, he observed, 'generally speaking History bears out the proposition that political revolutions have always been preceded by social and religious revolutions'. It was obviously in response to communist arguments informed by 'base and superstructure' that unless the economic (not political) structure of the society is changed the superstructure of caste would not change. This argument could be better faulted by showing that castes were not merely a religious or socio-cultural matter but as discussed before had an economic content as well. But Ambedkar, in his anxiety to disprove the communists' thesis, fell into their trap conceding that castes indeed were religious products and hence part of the superstructure. Also, there was no contention between religious and political in the communist argument; both being part of the superstructure; the base was supposed to comprise economic.

Ambedkar always thought that unless caste consciousness was killed, there might not be any germination of class-consciousness. The communists of his day with their doctrinaire approach to the problem had only contributed to the hardening of his opinions along these lines. If they had initiated a constructive dialogue and discussed the modalities of dealing with caste, his sequential reading of these revolutions perhaps could have been changed to a dialectical form. But that is a hypothetical thought. The current book, if he had completed it, would have cleared many such issues. His motivation to write such a book rather reflects a certain affinity between him and Marx. Ambedkar shared with Marx and with liberal Enlightenment thinkers a belief in progress, a conviction that history brought with it an advance in human welfare. In Marxist terms we can interpret this as the advance in the forces of production that brings with it an advance in human capacities; in liberal terms we can speak of an advance in freedom. Ambedkar also believed that human history is a history of progress, a forward movement and not simply a phase in endless cycles or final degeneration. He differed with Marx in interpreting the motive force of human history.

BRIDGING THE RIFT

It is my conviction that if the early Marxists had shunned their romantic ideas about revolution and doctrinaire approach to Marxism, and genuinely grappled with the Indian reality, the destiny of India and thereby the world would have been very different. They had the most advanced analytical tools of Marxism, which could be judiciously used to understand social realities. Marxism was a science of societies not an *ism* as it came to be termed. Although it denoted the collection of socio-eco-political theories expounded by Karl Marx and Friedrich Engels, it was not supposed to be confined to them. If there is contra evidence to its postulates, it should correct itself and still stay as Marxism. As Ernest Mandel remarked, 'Marxism is always open, always critical, always self-critical'.[101] Marx himself had explicated what he meant by Marxism. In 1883, Marx wrote to the French labour leader Jule Guesde and to Paul Lafargue (his son-in-law) – both of whom claimed to represent Marxist principles – accusing them of 'revolutionary phrase-mongering' and of denying the value of reformist struggle.[102] Marx made his famous remark that if their politics represented Marxism – '*cequ'il y a de certain c'estquemoi, je ne suis pas Marxiste*' (what is certain is that I myself am not a Marxist).[103] Unfortunately, many Marxists have not paid any heed to this distinctive characteristic of Marxism and treated it as a dogma or religion. American Marxist scholar Hal Draper pertinently remarked, 'there are few thinkers in modern history whose thought has been so badly misrepresented, by Marxists and anti-Marxists alike'.[104] He pertinently reminded communists of

[101] Ernest Mandel, Vanguard Parties (March 1983). https://www.marxists.org/archive/mandel/1983/03/vanguard.htm. [Last accessed: 29 November 2016]

[102] A dispute arose over a document jointly drafted by Marx and Guesde in May 1980, where in Marx had proposed a minimum political programme as a practical means of agitation around demands that were achievable within the framework of capitalism. Guesde and Lafargue took a very different view, calling it reformist that would lure workers away from radicalism. Guesde believed that the rejection of it would "free the proletariat of its last reformist illusions" Karl Marx and Jules Guesde 1880. See, *The Programme of the Parti Ouvrier*, https://www.marxists.org/archive/marx/works/1880/05/parti-ouvrier.htm. [Last accessed: 29 November 2016]

[103] Ibid.

[104] https://www.classle.net/#!/classle/book/marxs-thought/. Accessed: 29 Nov.

their folly in calling Ambedkar as reformist as though reforms were a taboo in Marxism.

In contrast to the Marxists, Ambedkar did not have even a reference to be guided by in his battle against the caste system, which was admittedly unique in the world. Instead of appreciating his struggle and bridging the ideological gap, the communists chose to ridicule him and called him names such as reactionary, reformist, and stooge of imperialism. The onus of creating and expanding the unfortunate rift between the two streams of the movement of the proletariat in the country should be squarely borne by the communists. After Ambedkar died, they began mending their attitude towards the struggle he built. For instance, in 1979, E.M.S. Namboodiripad placed the Marxian approach to the struggle against caste consciousness and caste oppression as a part of the class struggle:

> One has to realize that the building of India on modern democratic and secular lines requires an uncompromising struggle against the caste-based Hindu society and its culture. There is no question of secular democracy, not to speak of socialism, unless the very citadel of India's 'age-old' civilization and culture – the division of society into a hierarchy of castes – is broken. In other words, the struggle for radical democracy and socialism cannot be separated from the struggle against caste society.[105]

The same year B.T. Ranadive, regretted the fact that 'there has been a certain neglect in the ideological struggle against caste and

---

2016.

[105] *Economic and Political Weekly*, Annual Number, 1979, p. 347. For other writings of E.M.S. on class-caste relations, see *Problems of National Integration*, Calcutta: National Book Agency, 1966; *Kerala Yesterday, Today and Tomorrow*, Calcutta: NBA, 1968; and *Selected Writings*, Calcutta: NBA, 1982, vol. I; *History, Society and Land Relations*, New Delhi: LeftWord, 2010.

communalism', and that 'the common consciousness generated through the economic struggle cannot be pushed forward without such struggle and direct intervention of the movement on caste oppression'.[106] Three years later, in his book, *Class, Caste and Property Relations*, Ranadive strongly pleaded for the adoption of an anti-caste programme of struggle by all mass organizations:

> The decisive challenge of caste and untouchability has to be defeated by the leaders of the mass struggles by inculcating a strong anti-caste feeling among the fighting toilers – above all among the workers in the spirit of proletarian unity and solidarity. This can be achieved by strong ideological propaganda against the caste system and untouchability . . . . Then alone the mighty force of the united toilers will decisively strike for agrarian revolution, smashing the basis of caste distinctions and serfdom of the untouchables; then alone the democratic forces will open the way to political power and rapid industrialization on the basis of socialization of all means of production and usher in a casteless and classless society.[107]

Both E.M.S. Namboodiripad and B.T. Ranadive thus felt the urgent need for integrating the class struggle with the struggle against the caste system in India, and considered this integration to be essential for the success of the proletarian revolution and the establishment of people's democracy in this country. This ideological position of these stalwarts was reflected in a resolution of the Salkia Plenum of the CPI(M) in 1978, which stated that the ruling class took advantage of caste and communal divisions among the people, and emphasized the need for a mass struggle against casteism and communalism.

[106] Ibid., p. 355.

[107] B.T. Ranadive, *Caste, Class and Property Relations*, National Book Agency, Calcutta, 1982, Foreword.

This realization of the communists was perhaps too late as the rift by then had widened and deepened considerably. Notwithstanding, there have been bright spots in history where the communists and the Ambedkarite Dalits struggled together as a class. The land satyagraha in 1959 in the Khandesh and Marathwada region of Maharashtra, led by Dadasaheb Gaikwad, in which many communists went to jail along with Dalits, is a case in point. The rise of Dalit Panther had also created a hope of convergence between these two streams. The reason that these spots did not make a broad pattern *inter alia* is the lack of realization by these two movements that their goals really intersect and are not achievable without their unity. Their marginalization today is the unfortunate proof of this dictum, The way-out of this downward spin is to candidly admit the past mistakes and correct them in a spirit of self-criticism.

The Dalit movement is almost decimated by its leaders who made brokering of Dalit interests into an art form. Paradoxically, Ambedkar is used by the ruling classes in accelerating this process. He is reduced to be an inert icon devoid of its radical content that could be manipulated to win Dalit votes. All political parties today sing paeans to him. Communists were only feeling their way. Today, there is no communist outfit that is not acknowledging the importance of battling caste and Ambedkar's contribution to it. A few, however, have overcome their ideological hangover of the 'base and superstructure' and the fixated notion of imperialism, that pose hurdles in understanding Ambedkar. They need to rethink and get back to the basics of Marxism, not as a sect but as science.

The alienation of Ambedkar from communists was largely attributable to this misplaced ideological obsession of the communists. It has been skilfully capitalized by vested interests among the Dalits to keep them away from any shade of radicalism. While the follies of the communist were of their own creation, the propaganda among the Dalits of Ambedkar being against Marxism is not entirely of their own making; the might of the ruling classes is certainly promoting it. In the parliamentary context, the autonomous Dalit voice was decimated in the Poona Pact in colonial times, which the cunning of the ruling classes skilfully incorporated into independent India's constitution. Today, its aftermath is glaringly seen with all the so-called Dalit leaders being in the lap of the Hindutva forces, which Ambedkar battled against. They have aided the distortion of Ambedkar's thought to the extent that it would be difficult to recover his original radical self. As a result, there is no way to arrest the identitarian obsession that is growing among the Dalits. The younger generation of educated Dalits instead of analysing their history and contributing new directions to the Dalit movement, as Babasaheb Ambedkar had expected them to, are regressing to their old identities and unconsciously aiding the ruling classes.

The current times are depressing beyond narration. Capitalism has assumed a grotesque form of neoliberalism that is running roughshod all over the world, unleashing unprecedented crises on the entire lower strata of people. In the absence of a radical ideology to resist its onslaught, there has been a resurgence of identities and religious fundamentalism all over the world duly abetted by global capital, which has splintered people into infinite fragments. The communists ought to realise that much of it has been due to their own mishandling of Marxism. It is they who are responsible for their own marginalisation. Standing at this point, firstly, it must be realised by both Dalits as well as Communists that no *ism*, howsoever it might have worked in the past, is going to be applicable to the volatile contemporary and future world. The world is changing with an increasingly accelerated pace. Its essence may not be grasped by the frameworks that worked for its previous versions. These *isms* could only be beacons but the specific path shall have to be carved out by the people themselves in the concrete situation they find them in. With this realization the identitarian obsession should melt away. Second, they both must know they are natural allies; there is no revolution in India without the Dalits shouldering it and there is no annihilation of caste without the vast sections of the toiling masses owning it up. Third, the communists must realize that the onus is theirs to join hands with the Dalit masses and it must be genuine, beyond electoral logic. The Dalits should realise that politics based only on caste identities will only splinter them further to the glee of the ruling classes. Only their class unity sans caste is the path of their emancipation. Fourth, the communists should realise that revolutions are not a point concept but a line concept; the numerous tactical reforms that drive the revolutionary strategy, are themselves part of the revolution. The familiar models of revolutions were fundamentally misconceived and future revolutions are certainly not going to conform to them. The technological dimension would be overwhelming the future which on the one hand threatens human existence but on the other, drives towards socialism; the revolution is to decide which way it takes. And fifth and last, both must realize that there is no future for them without revolution.

May this publication of Babasaheb Ambedkar's incomplete writings inspire the Dalits and communists to complete this belated task to shape India's, and the world's future![108]

[108] I would thank my friend S.V. Rajadurai for pointing out certain errors in the original text and gratefully acknowledge his friendly assistance in revising it.

B.R. Ambedkar

India and Communism

CHAPTER 4

THE HINDU SOCIAL ORDER: ITS ESSENTIAL PRINCIPLES

I

What is the character of the Hindu Social Order? Is it a free social order? To answer this question, some idea of what constitutes a free social order is necessary. Fortunately, the matter is not one of controversy. Since the days of the French Revolution there is no difference as to the essentials of a free social order. There may be more but two are fundamental. Generally speaking, they are two. The first is that the individual is an end in himself and that the aim and object of society is the growth of the individual and the development of his personality. Society is not above the individual and if the individual has to subordinate himself to society, it is because such subordination is for his betterment and only to the extent necessary.

The second essential is that the terms of associated life between members of society must be regarded by consideration founded on liberty, equality and fraternity.

Why are these two essentials fundamental to a free social order?

Why must the individual be the end and not the means of all social purposes? For an answer to this question, it is necessary to realise what we precisely mean when we speak of the human person. Why should we sacrifice our most precious possessions and our lives to defend the rights of the human person? No better answer to this question can be found than what is given by Prof. Jacques Maritain. As Prof. Maritain in his essay on 'The Conquest of Freedom'[1] says,

> What do we mean precisely when we speak of the human person? When we say that a man is a person, we do not mean merely that he is an individual, in the sense that an atom, a blade of grass, a fly, or an elephant is an individual. Man is an individual who holds himself in hand by his intelligence and his will; he exists not merely in a physical fashion. He has spiritual super-existence through knowledge and love, so that he is, in a way, a universe in himself, a microcosmos, in which the great universe in its entirety can be encompassed through knowledge. By love he can give himself completely to beings who are to him, as it were, other selves. For this relation no equivalent can be found in the physical world. The human person possesses these characteristics because in the last analysis man, this flesh and these perishable bones which are animated and activated by a divine fire, exists 'from the womb to the grave' by virtue of the existence itself of his soul, which dominates time and death. Spirit is the root of personality. The notion of personality thus involves that of totality and independence, no matter how poor and crushed a person may

[1] *Freedom – Its Meaning* by Ruth Nanda Anshen, p. 214. [*Editor's Note*: Ambedkar's citation refers to Ruth Nanda Anshen, an American philosopher, who collected a series of texts in *Freedom: Its Meaning* in 1940. Ambedkar quotes from the essay by Jacques Maritain, a French Catholic philosopher. Maritain was a fierce anti-Communist.]

be, he is a whole, and as a person subsistent in an independent manner. To say that a man is a person is to say that in the depth of his being he is more a whole than a part and more independent than servile. It is to say that he is a minute fragment of matter that is at the same time a universe, a beggar who participates in the absolute being, mortal flesh whose value is external and a bit of straw – into which heaven enters. It is this metaphysical mystery that religious thought designates when it says that the person is the image of God. The value of the person, his dignity and rights, belong to the order of things naturally sacred which bear the imprint of the Father of Being, and which have in him the end of their movement.

Why is Equality essential? The best exposition of the subject is by Prof. Beard in his essay on 'Freedom in Political Thought' and I shall do no more than quote him. Says Prof. Beard,[2]

> The term 'Equality' is unfortunate, but no other word can be found as a substitute. Equality means 'exactly the same or equivalent in measure, amount, number, degree, value, or quality'. It is a term exact enough in physics and mathematics, but obviously inexact when applied to human beings. What is meant by writers who have gone deepest into the subject is that human beings possess, in degree and kind, fundamental characteristics that are common to humanity. These writers hold that when humanity is stripped of extrinsic goods and conventions incidental to time and place, it reveals essential characteristics so widely distributed as to partake of universality. Whether these characteristics be called primordial qualities, biological necessities, residues or any other name matters little. No one can truthfully deny that they do exist. It is easy to point

[2] *Freedom – Its Meaning*, pp. 11-13. [*Editor's Note*: The Professor Beard here is Charles A. Beard, a progressive American historian who understood class conflict to be the essential driver of history.]

out inequalities in physical strength, in artistic skill, in material wealth, or in mental capacity, but this too is a matter of emphasis. At the end it remains a fact that fundamental characteristics appear in all human beings. Their nature and manifestations are summed up in the phrase 'moral equality'. Emphasis must be placed on the term 'moral'. From time immemorial it has been the fashion of critics to point out the obvious facts that in physical strength, talents, and wealth, human beings are not equal. The criticism is both gratuitous and irrelevant. No rational exponent of moral equality has even disputed the existence of obvious inequalities among human beings, even when he has pointed out inequalities which may be ascribed to tyranny or institutional prescriptions. The Declaration of Independence [in the United States] does not assert that all men are equal; it proclaims that they are 'created' equal. In essence the phrase 'moral equality' asserts in ethical value, a belief to be sustained, and recognition of rights to be respected. Its validity cannot be demonstrated as a problem in mathematics can be demonstrated. It is asserted against inequalities in physical strength, talents, industry, and wealth. It denied that superior physical strength has a moral right to kill, eat, or oppress human beings merely because it is superior. To talents and wealth, the ideal of moral equality makes a similar denial of right. And indeed few can imagine themselves to have superior physical strength, talents and wealth will withhold from inferiors all moral rights. In such circumstances government and wealth would go to superior physical strength; while virtue and talents would serve the brute man, as accomplished Greek slaves served the whims, passions and desires to Roman conquerors. When the last bitter word of criticism has been uttered against the ideal of moral equality, there remains something in it which all, except things, must accept and in practice do accept, despite their sneers and protests. A society without any respect for human personalities is a band of robbers.

Why is Fraternity essential?

Fraternity is the name for the disposition of an individual to treat men as the object of reverence and love and the desire to be in unity with his fellow beings. This statement is well expressed by Paul when he said 'Of one blood are all nations of men, There is neither Jew nor Greek, neither bond nor free, neither male nor female; for yet are all one in Christ Jesus.' Equally well was it expressed when the Pilgrim Fathers on their landing at Plymouth said: 'We are knit together as a body in the most sacred covenant of the Lord . . . by virtue of which we hold ourselves tied to all care of each others' good and of the whole.' These sentiments are of the essence of fraternity. Fraternity strengthens societies and gives to each individual a stronger personal interest in practically consulting the welfare of others. It leads him to identify his feelings more and more with their good, or at least with an even greater degree of practical consideration for it. With a disposition to fraternity he comes as though instructively to be conscious of himself as being one who of course pays a regard to others. The good of others becomes to him a thing naturally and necessarily to be attended to like any of the physical conditions of our existence. Where people do not feel that entireness of sympathy with all others, concordance in the general direction of their conduct is impossible. For a person in whom social feeling is not developed cannot but bring himself to think of the rest of his fellow-beings as rivals struggling with him for the means of happiness when he must endeavour to defeat in order that he may succeed in himself.

What is Liberty and why is it essential in a free social order?

Liberty falls under two classes. There is civil liberty and there is political liberty. Civil liberty refers to (I) liberty of movement which is another name for freedom from arrest without due process of law (2) liberty of speech (which of course includes liberty of thought, liberty of reading, writing and discussion) and (3) liberty of action.

The first kind of liberty is of course fundamental. Not only fundamental it is also most essential. About its value, there can be no manner of doubt. The second kind of liberty which may be called freedom of opinion is important for many reasons. It is a necessary condition of all progress intellectual, moral, political and social. Where it does not exist the status quo becomes stereotyped and all originality even the most necessary is discouraged. Liberty of action means doing what one likes to do. It is not enough that liberty of action should be formal. It must be real. So understood, liberty of action means effective power to do specific things. There is no freedom where there are no means of taking advantage of it. Real liberty of action exists only where exploitation has been annihilated, where no suppression of one class by another exists, where there is no unemployment, no poverty and where a person is free from the fear of losing his job, his home and his food as a consequence of his action.

Political liberty consists in the right of the individual to share in the framing of laws and in the making and unmaking of governments. Governments are instituted for securing to men certain unalienable rights such as life, liberty and pursuit of happiness. Government must, therefore, derive its powers from those whose rights it is charged with the duty to protect. This is what is meant when it is said that the existence, power and authority of the Government must be derived from the consent of the governed. Political liberty is really a deduction from the principle of human personality and equality. For it implies that all political authority is derived from the people that the people are capable of directing and controlling their public as well as private lives to ends determined by themselves and by none else.

These two tenets of a free social order are integrally connected. They are inseverable. Once the first tenet is admitted, the second tenet automatically follows. Once the sacredness of human personality is admitted the necessity of liberty, equality and fraternity must also be admitted as the proper climate for the development of personality.

II

How far does the Hindu social order recognise these tenets? The inquiry is necessary. For it is only in so far as it recognizes these tenets that it will have the title to be called a free social order.

Does the Hindu social order recognise the individual? Does it recognise his distinctiveness his moral responsibility? Does it recognise him as an end in himself, as a subject not merely of disabilities but also of rights even against the State? As a starting point for the discussion of the subject one may begin by referring to the words of the Exodus where Jehovah says to Ezekiel,

> Behold! all souls are mine; as the soul of the Father, so also the soul of the son is mine; the soul that sinneth, it shall die . . . the son shall not bear the iniquity of the Father, neither shall the father bear the iniquity of the son; the righteousness of the righteous shall be upon him, and the wickedness of the wicked upon him.[3]

Here is emphasized the distinctiveness of the individual and his moral responsibility. The Hindu social order does not recognise the individual as a centre of social purpose. For the Hindu social order is based primarily on class or Varna and not on individuals. Originally and formally the Hindu social order

[3] [*Editor's Note*: Ezekiel, 18: 4, The Bible.]

recognized four classes: (1) Brahmans, (2) Kshatriyas (3) Vaishyas and (4) Shudras. Today it consists of five classes, the fifth being called the Panchamas or Untouchables. The unit of Hindu society is not the individual Brahman or the individual Kshatriya or the individual Vaishya or the individual Shudra or the individual Panchama. Even the family is not regarded by the Hindu social order as the unit of society except for the purposes of marriage and inheritance. The unit of Hindu society is the class or Varna to use the Hindu technical name for class. In the Hindu social order, there is no room for individual merit and no consideration of individual justice. If the individual has a privilege it is not because it is due to him personally. The privilege goes with the class, and if he is found to enjoy it, it is because he belongs to that class. Contrawise, if an individual is suffering from a wrong, it is not because he by his conduct deserves it. The disability is the disability imposed upon the class and if he is found to be labouring under it, it is because he belongs to that class.

Does the Hindu social order recognize fraternity? The Hindus like the Christians and the Muslims do believe that men are created by God. But while the Christians and the Muslims accept this as the whole truth the Hindus believe that this is only part of the truth. According to them, the whole truth consists of two parts. The first part is that men are created by God. The second part is that God created different men from different parts of his divine body. The Hindus regard the second part as more important and more fundamental than the first.

The Hindu social order is based on the doctrine that men are created from the *different* parts of the divinity and therefore the view expressed by Paul or the Pilgrim Fathers has no place in it. The Brahman is no brother to the Kshatriya because the former is born from the mouth of the divinity while the latter is from the arms. The Kshatriya is no brother to the Vaishya because the former is born from the arms and the latter from his thighs. As no one is a brother to the. other, no one is the keeper of the other.

The doctrine that the different classes were created from different parts of the Divine body has generated the belief that it must be divine will that they should remain separate and distinct. It is this belief which has created in the Hindu an instinct to be different, to be separate and to be distinct from the rest of his fellow Hindus. Compare the following rules in the *Manu Smriti* regarding the Upanayan or the Investiture of a body with the sacred thread:

> II. 36. 'In the eighth year after conception, one should perform the initiation (Upanayan) of a Brahman in the eleventh after conception (that) of a Kshatriya but in the twelfth that of a Vaishya'.
>
> II. 41. 'Let students according to the order (of their castes), wear (as upper dressed) the skins of black antelope, spotted deer, and he-goats and (lower garments) made of hemp, flax or wool'.
>
> II. 42. 'The girdle of a Brahmana shall consist of a triple cord of Munga grass, smooth and soft (that) of a Kshatriya, of a bowstring, made of Murva fibres (that) of a Vaishya of hempen threads'.
>
> II. 43. 'If Munga grass (and soforth) be not procurable, (the girdles) may be made of kusa, Asmantaka, and Balbaga (fibres) with a single threefold knot, or with three or five (knots) according to the custom of the family'.
>
> II. 44. 'The sacrificial string of a Brahmana shall be made of cotton (shall be) twisted to the right, (and consist) of three threads, that of a Kshatriya of hempen threads, and that of a Vaishya of woollen threads'.
>
> II. 45. 'A Brahamana shall carry according to sacred law a staff of Bilva or Palasa, a Kshatriya of Vata or Khadira; and a Vaishya of Pillu or Udumbara'.
>
> II. 46. 'The staff of a Brahmana shall be made of such length as to

> reach the end of his hair; that of a Kshatriya to reach his forehead; and that of a Vaishya to reach the tip of his nose'.
>
> II. 48. 'Having taken a staff according to his choice having worshipped the Sun and walked round the fire, turning his right hand towards it (the student) should beg alms according to the prescribed rule'.
>
> II. 49. 'An initiated Brahmana should beg, beginning his request with the word lady (bhavati); a Kshatriya placing the word lady in the middle, but a Vaishya placing it at the end of the formula'.

On reading this one may well ask the reasons for such distinctions. The above rules refer to students or what are called Brahmacharis ready to enter upon the study of the Vedas. Why should there be these distinctions? Why should the ages of Upanayana of the Brahman boy differ from that of the Kshatriya or Vaishya? Why should their garments be of different kind? Why should their materials of girdle cords be different? Why should the material of strings be different? Why should their staves be of different trees? Why should their staves differ in length? Why in uttering the formula for asking alms they should place the word 'Bhavati' in different places? These differences are neither necessary nor advantageous. The only answer is that they are the result of the Hindu instinct to be different from his fellow which has resulted from the belief of people being innately different owing to their being created from different parts of the divine body.

It is also the Hindu instinct due to the same belief never to overlook a difference if it does exist but to emphasize it, recognize it and to blazen it forth. If there is caste its existence must be signalized by a distinguishing head-dress and by a distinguishing name. If there is a sect it must have its headmark. There are ninety-two sects in India. Each has a separate mark of itself. To invent ninety-two marks each one different from the other is a colossal business. The very impossibility of it would have made the most ingenious person to give up the task. Yet, the Hindus have accomplished it as may be seen from the pictorial representation of these marks given by Moor in his *Hindu Pantheon*.[4]

The most extensive and wild manifestation of this spirit of isolation and separation is of course the caste-system. It is understandable that caste in a single number cannot exist. Caste can exist only in plural number. There can be castes. But there cannot be such a thing as a caste. But granting that theoretically castes must exist, in plural number how many castes should there be? Originally, there were four only. Today, how many are there? It is estimated that the total is not less than two thousand. It might be three thousand. This is not the only staggering aspect of this fact. There are others. Castes are divided into sub-castes. Their number is legion. The total population of the Brahman castes is about a crore and a half. But there are one thousand eight hundred and eighty-six sub-castes of Brahman caste!! In the Punjab alone, the Saraswat Brahmans are divided into four hundred and sixty-nine sub-castes. The Kayasthas of Punjab are divided into eight hundred and ninety sub-castes!! One could go on giving figures to show this infinite process of splitting social life into small fragments. The splitting process has made a social life quite impossible. It has made the castes split into such small fragments that it has marital relationship consistent with the rule of excluded degrees quite impossible. Some of the Baniya sub-castes count no more than hundred families. They are so interrelated they find it extremely difficult to marry within their castes without transgressing the rules of consanguinity.

It is noteworthy that small excuses suffice to bring about this splitting of castes into sub-castes. Castes become sub-divided into

[4] [*Editor's Note*: Edward Moor's *Hindu Pantheon* was published in London in 1810. It was a primer for an English audience on Hinduism, lavishly illustrated including by William Blake.]

sub-castes by reason of change of location, change of occupation, change in social practices, change due to pollution, changes due to increased prosperity, changes due to quarrel and changes due to change of religion. Mr. Blunt has given many instances to illustrate this tendency among the Hindus. There is no space to reproduce all except one, which shows how ordinary quarrels lead to the splitting one caste into sub-castes. As stated by Mr. Blunt:[5]

> In Lucknow there was a sub-caste of Khatika consisting of three *ghols* or groups, known as Manikpur, Jaiswala and Dalman. They inter-married, ate together, and met together in panchayat under the presidency of their Chaudharis or headmen. Twenty years ago each group had one Chaudhri, but now Jaiswala have three and Manikpur two. The quarrel was as follows. Firstly a woman (her ghol is not given) peddled fruit about the streets. The brethren ordered her to desist from the practice, which is derogatory to the caste's dignity; women should only sell in shops. Her husband and she proved contumacious; and finally their own ghol, acting singly, outcasted the man. The Dalmu ghol, however, dissenting from this action admitted the husband to communion with themselves upon payment of a fine of Rs. 80 in lieu of excommunication. Secondly a man (the ghol, again is not given) was excommunicated by his own ghol, acting alone; and while his case was under trial, the Jaiswala Chaudhri invited him to dinner by mistake. Thereupon, the three ghols, acting in concert, fined the Chaudhri Rs. 30. Lastly, fines had accumulated and it was decided to hold a Katha (sacred recitation). The Dalmu Chaudhri said he preferred to have his share of money; but the Manikpur Chaudhri (who seems to have kept the joint

[5] Blunt, 'The Caste System of Northern India', pp. 51-56. [*Editor's Note*: Ambedkar cites the work of Sir E.A.H. Blunt, an imperial civil servant, who was the Superintendent of the Census Operation in the United Provinces. He began to write the book in 1913, based on his Census work. It was not completed till 1930 and published the next year by Oxford University Press.]

purse) refused, taking up the attitude that there was going to be a Katha to which the Dalmu people could come or not as they liked. The matter at this stage was brought into court; meanwhile the three ghols ceased to inter-marry, so that one endogamous sub-caste split into three quarrels, ghol was pitted against ghol.

If in any caste a group should adopt some new or unusual worship of which other members do not approve, one would expect that group to break off and become an endogamous sub-caste. That such sub-castes are uncommon is due to the tolerance about what and with whom he eats and whom he marries. We do, however, find that the Mahabhiras and Panchipriya sub-castes amongst Telis, Koris and the Namakshalis amongst Barhais, Bhangis and Kadheras.

How do these castes behave towards one another. Their guiding principle is 'be separate', 'do not intermarry,' 'do not interdine' and 'do not touch'. Mr. Blunt has well described the situation when he says,

> A Hindu sits down to a meal either alone or with his caste fellows. The women cannot eat with the men; they wait till their lords have finished. So long as the meal or a part of it consists of Kachcha food (as it usually does, since Chapatis appear at most meals), the man must dine with the precautions of a magic ceremony. He sits within a square marked off on the ground (chauka) inside which is the Chulha or cooking place. Should a stranger's shadow fall upon this square, all food cooked within it is polluted and must be thrown away. In camp, Hindu servants may be seen, each well apart from the rest, each within his own chauka, cooking his food upon his own mud oven and eating alone . . .
>
> Rules regarding the acceptance of water are on the whole the same as those regarding the acceptance of a pakka food, but with a tendency to greater laxity. The vessel in which the water is contained

affects the question. A high caste man will allow a low caste man to fill his lota (drinking vessel) for him; but he will not drink from the lota of that low caste man. Or a high caste man will give anybody (save Untouchables) a drink, by pouring water from his own lota into that of the drinker; all the men employed at stations to supply railway travellers with water are Barhais, Baris, Bharbhunjas, Halwais, Kahars, and Nais; and of course from higher castes still.

Rules regarding smoking are stricter. It is very seldom that a man will smoke with anybody but a caste fellow; the reason, no doubt is that smoking with a man usually involves smoking his pipe, and this involves much closer contact even than eating food which he has prepared. So stringent is this rule, indeed, that the fact that Jats, Ahirs, and Gujars will smoke together has been regarded as a ground for supposing that they are closely akin. Some castes, the Kayastha for instance, differentiates between smoking in narial fashion in which the hands are closed round the pipe and the smoke is drawn in without putting the stem actually in the mouth – and smoking in the usual way. Little need be said on the subject of vessels. There are rules laying down what sort of vessels should be made, but they are rather religious than social. Hindus must use brass or alloy (although the use of alloy is hedged about by numerous and minute injunctions, and if such vessels become impure, the only remedy is to get them remoulded). The risk of pollution makes it imperative for every man to have a few vessels of his own. The minimum consists of a lota (drinking vessel), batna (cooking pot), and thali (dish). Better class folk add a Katora (spoon) and Gagra (Water pot). For feasts, the brotherhood usually keep a set of larger vessels of all kinds, which they lend to the host; these are bought with the proceeds of fines, and are common property.[6]

[6] In the Northern India the bar to eating together applies only when the food is kachcha food. In Southern India the bar is complete and applies even when the food it pucca food. Kachcha food is food cooked in water. Pacca food is food cooked in ghee.

What fraternity can there be in a social order based upon such sentiments? Far from working in a spirit of fraternity the mutual relations of the castes are fratricidal. Class-consciousness, class struggle and class war are supposed to be ideologies which came into vogue from the writings of Karl Marx. This is a complete mistake. India is the land which has experienced class consciousness, class struggle. Indeed, India is the land where there has been fought a class war between Brahmans and Kshatriyas[7] which lasted for several generations and which was fought so hard and with such virulence that it turned but to be a war of extermination.

It must not be supposed that the fratricidal spirit has given place to a spirit of fraternity. The same spirit of separation marks the Hindu social order today as may be seen from what follows:

Each class claims a separate origin. Some claim origin from a Rishi or from a hero. But in each case it is a different Rishi or a different hero having nothing to do with the Rishis and heroes claimed by other castes as their progenitors. Each caste is engaged in nothing but establishing for itself a status superior to that of another caste. This is best illustrated by rules of hypercommensality and rules of hypergamy. As pointed out by Mr. Blunt,[8]

> It is essential to realize that in respect of the cooking taboo, the criterion is the caste of the person who cooks the food, not the caste of the person who offers it. It follows, therefore, that a high caste Hindu can eat the food of a man of any caste, however low, if his host possesses a cook of suitable caste. And that is why so many cooks are Brahmins. The Hindu draws a distinction between kachcha food, which is cooked in water and pucca food which is cooked with ghee

[7] See my book 'Who were the Shudras?' [B.R. Ambedkar, *Who Were the Shudras?* Bombay: Thacker & Co., 1949].

[8] 'The Caste System of Northern India', pp. 89-90. [E.A.H. Blunt, *The Caste System of Northern India*, London: Humphrey Milford, Oxford University Press, 1931].

(clarified butter). This distinction depends on the principle that ghee, like all the products of the sacred cow, protects from impurity, and since such protection is the object of all food taboos, this convenient fiction enables the Hindu to be less particular in the case of pucca food than of kachcha food, and to relax his restrictions accordingly.

Speaking of hypergamy, Mr. Blunt[9] says,

> The custom of hypergamy introduces an important modification into the marriage laws of many castes. Where it prevails, the exogamous groups are classified according to their social position; and whilst a group of highest rank will take brides from it, it will not give brides to a group of lower rank. The law is found most highly developed amongst Rajputs but it is observed by many other castes . . . Indeed amongst all Hindus there is probably a tendency towards hypergamy.

What is it that has behind these rules regarding hyper-commensality and hypergamy? Nothing else but the spirit of high and low. All castes are infested with that spirit and there is no caste which is free from it. The Hindu social order is a ladder of castes placed one above the other together representing an ascending scale of hatred and a descending scale of contempt.

This spirit has exhibited itself in the proverbs coined by one caste with the object of lampooning another caste. It has given rise even to literature by authors of low castes suggesting filthy origin of the so-called high caste. The Sahyadrikhand is the best illustration of it. It is one of the Puranas which form part of the Hindu sacred literature. It is a Purana of a style quite different from the traditional puranas. It deals with the origin of the different castes. In doing so, it assigns noble origin to other castes while it assigns to the Brahman caste the filthiest origin.

[9] 'The Caste System of Northern India', ibid.

Does the Hindu social order recognise equality? The answer must be in the negative. That men are born equal is a doctrine which is repugnant to the Hindu social order. In the spiritual sense it treats the doctrine as false. According to the Hindu social order though it is true that men are the children of Prajapati the Creator of the Universe, they are not equal on that account. For, they were created from the different parts of the body of Prajapati. The Brahmans were created from the mouth, the Kshatriyas from the arms, the Vaishyas from his thighs and Shudras from his feet. The limbs from which they were created being of unequal value the men thus created are as unequal. In the biological sense, the Hindu social order does not bother to examine whether the doctrine is founded in a fact. If it was not a fact, i.e., men were not equal in their character and natural endowments of character and intelligence so much the better. On the other hand, if it was a fact, i.e., men were equal in character and natural endowments, so much the worse for the doctrine. The Hindu social order is indifferent to the doctrine as a fact. It is equally indifferent to it as an ethical principle. It refuses to recognise that men no matter how profoundly they differ as individuals in capacity and character, are equally entitled as human beings to consideration and respect and that the well-being of a society is likely to be increased if it so plans its organization that, whether their powers are great or small, all its members may be equally enabled to make the best of such powers as they possess. It will not allow equality of circumstances, institutions and manner of life. It is against equalitarian temper.

III

If the Hindu social order is not based on equality and fraternity, what are the principles on which it is based? There is only one answer to this question. Though few will be able to realize what they are, there is no doubt as to their nature and effect on Hindu society. The Hindu social order is reared on three principles. Among these the first and foremost is the principle of graded inequality.

That the principle of graded inequality is a fundamental principle is beyond controversy. The four classes are not on horizontal plane, different but equal. They are on vertical plane. Not only different, but unequal in status, one standing above the other. In the scheme of Manu, the Brahman is placed at the first in rank. Below him is the Kshatriya. Below the Kshatriya is the Vaishya. Below Vaishya is the Shudra and below Shudra is the Ati-Shudra or the Untouchable. This order of precedence among the classes is not merely conventional. It is spiritual, moral and legal. There is no sphere of life which is not regulated by this principle of graded inequality.

One can substantiate this by numerous illustrations from the *Manu Smriti.* I will take four illustrations to prove the point. They will be the law of slavery, law of marriage, law of punishment and law of Samskaras and law of Sanyas. The Hindu law recognised slavery as a legal institution. Manu Smriti recognised seven kinds of slaves. Narada Smriti recognised fifteen kinds of slaves. These differences as to the number of slaves and the classes under which they fall is a matter of no importance. What is important is to know who could enslave whom. On this point, the following citations from the Narada Smriti and the Yajnavalkya Smriti are revealing:

> Narada Smriti: V. 39. 'In the inverse order of four castes slavery is not ordained except where a man violates the duties peculiar to his caste. Slavery (in that respect) is analogous to the condition of a wife'.
> Yajnavalkya Smriti: XVI. 183 (2). 'Slavery is in the descending order of the Varnas and not in the ascending order'.

Recognition of slavery was bad enough. But if the rule of slavery had been left free to take its own course it would have had at least one beneficial effect. It would have been a leveling force. The foundation of caste would have been destroyed. For under it, a Brahman might have become the slave of the Untouchables and the Untouchables would have become the masters of the Brahman. But it was seen that unfettered slavery was an equalitarian principle and an attempt was made to nullify it. Manu and his successors therefore while recognising slavery ordain that it shall not be recognized in its inverse order to the Varna system. That means that a Brahman may become the slave of another Brahman. But he shall not be the slave of a person of another Varna, i.e., of the Kshatriya, Vaishya, Shudra, or Ati-Shudra. On the other hand, a Brahman may hold as his slave anyone belonging to the four Varnas. A Kshatriya can have a Kshatriya, Vaishya, Shudra and Ati-Shudra as his slaves but not one who is a Brahman. A Vaishya can have a Vaishya, Shudra and Ati-Shudra as his slaves but not one who is a Brahman or a Kshatriya. A Shudra can hold a Shudra and an Ati-Shudra, as his slaves but not one who is a Brahman, Kshatriya or a Vaishya. Ati-Shudra can hold an Ati-Shudra as his slave but not one who is a Brahman, Kshatriya, Vaishya or Shudra.

Another illustration of this principle of graded inequality is to be found in the laws of marriage. Manu says,

> III. 12. 'For the first marriage of the twice-born classes, a woman of the same class is recommended but for such as are impelled by inclination to marry again, women in the direct order of the classes are to be preferred'.
>
> III. 13. 'A Shudra woman only must be the wife of a Shudra; she and a Vaishya, of a Vaishya; they two and a Kshatriya of a Kshatriya; those three and a Brahmani of a Brahman'.

Manu is of course opposed to inter-marriage. His injunction is for each class to marry within his class. But he does recognize marriage outside the defined class. Here again, he is particularly careful not to allow inter-marriage to do harm to his principle of inequality among classes. Like slavery he permits inter-marriage but not in the inverse order. 'A Brahman when marrying outside his class may marry any woman from any of the classes below him. A Kshatriya is free to marry a woman from the two classes next below him, namely, the Vaishya and Shudra but must not marry a woman from the Brahman class which is above him. A Vaishya is free to marry a woman from the Shudra class which is next below him. But he cannot marry a woman from the Brahman and the Kshatriya class which are above him.'

The third illustration is to be found in the Rule of Law as enunciated by Manu. First as to treatment to be given to witnesses. According to Manu, they are to be sworn as follows,

> VIII. 87. 'In the forenoon let the judge, being purified, severally call on the twice-born, being purified also, to declare the truth, in the presence of some image, a symbol of the divinity and of Brahmans, while the witnesses turn their faces either to the north, or to the east'.

> VIII. 88. 'To a Brahman he must begin with saying 'Declare'; to a Kshatriya, with saying 'Declare the truth'; to a Vaishya admonishing him by mentioning his kine, grain or gold; to a Shudra, threatening him with the guilt of every crime that causes loss of caste'.

Take the punishment of offences as laid down by Manu. To begin with, punishment for defamation,

> VIII. 267. 'A soldier, defaming a priest, shall be fined a hundred panas; merchant thus offending, a hundred and fifty, or two hundred;

but for such an offence a mechanic or servile man shall be whipped'.
VIII. 268. 'A priest shall be fined fifty if he slanders a soldier; twenty-five if a merchant and twelve if he slanders a man of the servile class'.

Take the offence of insults. The punishment prescribed by Manu is as follows,

VIII. 270. 'A Shudra who insults a Dvija with gross invectives, ought to have his tongue slit for he sprang from the lowest part of Brahma'.
VIII. 271. 'If he mentions their names and classes with contumely, as if he says, 'Oh Devadatta, thou refuse of Brahman'; an iron nail, ten fingers long, shall be thrust red hot into his mouth'.
VIII. 272. 'Should he, through pride, give instructions to Brahmans concerning their duty; let the king order some hot oil to be dropped into his mouth and his ear'.

Punishment for the offence of abuse. Manu says,

VIII. 276. 'For mutual abuse by a Brahman and a Kshatriya, this fine must be imposed by a learned king; the lowest on the Brahman and the middlemost on the soldier'.
VIII. 277. 'A Vaishya and a Shudra must be punished exactly in the same manner according to their respective castes, except the slitting of the tongue of the Shudras. This is the fixed rule of punishment'.

Punishment for the offence of assault. Manu propounds,

VIII. 279. 'With whatever limb a Shudra shall assault or hurt a Dvija that limb of his shall be cut off, this is in accordance of Manu'.

Punishment for the offence of arrogance. According to Manu,

VIII. 281. 'A Shudra who shall insolently place himself on the same seat with a man of high caste, shall either be branded on his hip and be banished or the King shall cause a gash to be made on his buttock'.
VIII. 282. 'Should he spit on him through pride, the king shall order both his lips to be gashed; should he urine on him, his penis; should he break wind against him, his anus'.
VIII. 283. 'If he seizes the Brahman by the locks or likewise if he takes him by the feet, let the king unhesitatingly cut off his hands, or by the beard, or by the throat or by the scrotum'.

Punishment for the offence of adultery. Says Manu,

VIII. 359. 'A man who is not a Brahman who commits actual adultery ought to suffer death; for the wives, indeed of all the four classes must ever be most especially guarded'.
VIII. 366. 'A Shudra who makes love to a damsel of high birth, ought to be punished corporally; but he who addresses a maid of equal rank, shall give the nuptial present and marry her, if her father desires it'.
VIII. 374. 'A Shudra having an adulterous connection with a woman of a twice-born class, whether guarded at home or unguarded shall thus be punished in the following manner; if she was unguarded, he shall lose the part offending and all his property; if guarded everything even his life'.
VIII. 375. 'For adultery with a guarded Brahman a Vaishya shall forfeit all his wealth after imprisonment for a year; a Kshatriya shall be fined a thousand panas, and he be shaved with the urine of an ass'.
VIII. 376. 'But if a Vaishya or Kshatriya commits adultery with an unguarded Brahman, the king shall only fine the Vaishya five hundred panas and the Kshatriya a thousand'.
VIII. 377. 'But even these two however, it they commit that offence with a Brahmani not only guarded but the wife of an eminent man,

shall be punished like a Shudra or be burned in a fire of dry grass or reeds'.

VIII. 382. 'If a Vaishya approaches a guarded female of the Kshatriya or a Kshatriya a guarded Vaishya-woman, they both deserve the same punishment as in the case of an unguarded Brahman female'.

VIII. 383. 'But a Brahman, who shall commit adultery with a guarded woman of those two classes, must be fined a thousand panas, and for the offending with a Shudra woman the fine of a thousand panas on a Kshatriya or Vaishya'.

VIII. 384. 'For adultery by a Vaishya with a woman of the Kshatriya classes, if guarded, the fine is five hundred; but a Kshatriya for committing adultery on a Vaishya woman must be shaved with urine or pay the fine just mentioned'.

How strange is the contrast between Hindu and non-Hindu criminal jurisprudence! How inequality is writ large in Hinduism as seen in its criminal jurisprudence! In a Penal Code charged with the spirit of justice we find two things – a section dealing with defining the crime and a section prescribing a rational form of punishment for breach of it and a rule that all offenders are liable to the same penalty. In Manu, what do we find? First an irrational system of punishment. The punishment for a crime is inflicted on the origin concerned in the crime such as belly, tongue, nose, eyes, ears, organs of generation etc., as if the offending organ was sentient having a will for its own and had not been merely a servant of a human being. Second feature of Manu's Penal Code is the inhuman character of the punishment which has no proportion to the gravity of the offence. But the most striking feature of Manu's Penal Code which stands out in all its nakedness is the inequality of punishment for the same offence. Inequality designed not merely to punish the offender but to protect also the dignity and to maintain the baseness of the parties coming to a Court of Law to seek justice; in other words to maintain the social inequality on which his whole scheme is founded.

The principle of graded inequality has been carried into the economic field. 'From each according to his ability; to each according to his need' is not the principle of Hindu social order.[10] The principle of the Hindu social order is: 'From each according to his need. To each according to his nobility'.[11] Supposing an officer was distributing dole to a famine stricken people. He would be bound to give greater dole to a person of high birth than he would to a person of low birth. Supposing an officer was levying taxation. He would be bound to assess a person of high birth at a lower rate than he would to a person of low birth. The Hindu social order does not recognise equal need, equal work or equal ability as the basis of reward for labour. Its motto is that in regard to the distribution of the good things of life those who are reckoned as the highest must get the most and the best and those who are classed as the lowest must accept the least and the worst.

Nothing more seems to be necessary to prove that the Hindu social order is based on the principle of graded inequality. It

[10] [*Editor's Note*: Here Ambedkar quotes the line made famous in 1851 by the French socialist Louis Blanc, but then used most famously by Karl Marx in his 1875 *Critique of the Gotha Program*, where Marx wrote, 'In a higher phase of communist society, after the enslaving subordination of the individual to the division of labour, and therewith also the antithesis between mental and physical labour, has vanished; after labour has become not only a means of life but life's prime want; after the productive forces have also increased with the all-around development of the individual, and all the springs of co-operative wealth flow more abundantly – only then can the narrow horizon of bourgeois right be crossed in its entirety and society inscribe on its banners: *From each according to his ability, to each according to his needs*!']

[11] The illustrations given are not merely drawn from imagination. They are facts of history. The differentiation between high and low was recognised by law in the time of the Peshwas. The differentiation about dole exists even now in the Bombay Presidency and was defended by a Congress Minister.

pervades all departments of social life. Every side of social life is protected against the danger of equality.

The second principle on which the Hindu social order is founded is that of fixity of occupations for each class and continuance thereof by heredity. This is what Manu says about occupations of the four classes.

> I. 87. 'But in order to protect this universe, He, the most resplendent one, assigned separate (duties and) occupations, to those who sprang from his mouth, arms, thighs and feet'.
>
> I. 88. 'To Brahmanas he assigned teaching and studying (the Veda) sacrificing for their own benefit and for others, giving and accepting (of alms)'.
>
> I. 89. 'The Kshatriya he commanded to protect the people, to bestow gifts to offer sacrifices to study (the Veda) and to abstain from attaching himself to sensual pleasures. The Vaishya to tend cattle to bestow gifts to offer sacrifices to study (the Veda) and to abstain from attaching himself to sensual pleasures'.
>
> I. 91. 'One occupation only the Lord prescribed to the Shudra, to serve meekly even these (other) three castes'.

These rules regarding the occupations of the different classes are further amplified by Manu as will be seen from the following citations from his Smriti,

> I. 88. 'To Brahmans he (Swayambhu Manu) assigned the duties of reading the Veda, of teaching it, of sacrificing, of assisting others to sacrifice, of giving alms if they be rich, and if indigent of receiving of gifts'.
>
> I. 89. 'To defend the people, to give alms, to sacrifice, to read the Veda, to shun the allurements of sensual gratification, are in a few words, the duties of a Kshatnya'.

I. 90. 'To keep herds of cattle, to bestow largeness, to sacrifice, to read the scriptures, to carry on trade, to lend at interest, and to cultivate land are prescribed or permitted to a Vaishya'.

I. 91. 'One principal duty the supreme Ruler assigns to a Shudra; namely, to serve the before mentioned classes, without depreciating their worth'.

X. 74. 'Let such Brahmans as are intent on the means of attaining the supreme godhead, and firm in their own duties, completely perform in order, the six following acts'.

X. 75. 'Reading the Vedas, the teaching others to read them, sacrificing, and assisting others to sacrifice, giving to the poor if themselves have enough, and accepting gifts from the virtuous if themselves are poor, are the six prescribed acts of the firstborn class'.

X. 76. 'But, among those six acts of a Brahman three are his means of subsistence; assisting to sacrifice, teaching the Vedas and receiving gifts from a pure handed giver'.

X. 77. 'Three acts of duty cease with the Brahman and belong not to the Kshatriya, teaching the Vedas, officiating at a sacrifice and thirdly receiving presents'.

X. 78. 'Those three are also (by the fixed rule of law) forbidden to the Vaishya since Manu, the Lord of all men, prescribed not those acts to the two classes, military and commercial'.

X. 79. 'The means of subsistence peculiar to the Kshatriya are bearing arms, either held for striking or missile; to the Vajshya, merchandise, attending on cattle, and agriculture; but with a view to the next life, the duties of both are alms giving, reading and sacrificing'.

Every member must follow the trade assigned to the class to which he belongs. It leaves no scope for individual choice, individual inclination. An individual under the Hindu social order is bound to the profession of his ancestor. It is an inexorable law from which he cannot escape.

The principle does not stop with fixity of occupation. It grades the several occupations in terms of respectability. This is what Manu says,

> X. 80. 'Among the several occupations for gaining a livelihood the most commendable respectively for the Brahmans, Kshatriyas and the Vaishyas are the teaching of the Vedas, defending the people and trade'.

The third principle on which the Hindu social order is founded is the fixation of people within their respective classes. There is nothing strange or peculiar in the fact that the Hindu social order recognizes classes. There are classes everywhere and no society is without them. Families, cliques, clubs, political parties, nay communities, gangs engaged in criminal conspiracies, business corporations which prey upon the public are to be found in all societies in all parts of the world. Even a free social order will not be able to get rid of the classes. What a free social order aims to do is to prevent isolation and exclusiveness being regarded by the classes as an ideal to be followed. For so long as the classes do not practise isolation and exclusiveness they are only non-social in their relations towards one another. Isolation and exclusiveness make them anti-social and inimical towards one another. Isolation makes for rigidity of class-consciousness, for institutionalizing social life and for the dominance of selfish ideals within the classes. Isolation makes life static, continues the separation into a privileged and underprivileged, masters and servants.

Not so much the existence of classes as the spirit of isolation and exclusiveness which is inimical with a free social order. What a free social order endeavors to do is to maintain all channels of social endosmosis. This is possible only when the classes are free to share in an extensive number of common interests, undertakings and expenses, have a large number of values in common, when there is a free play back and forth, when they have an equable opportunity to receive and to take from others. Such social contacts must and does dissolve custom, makes for an alert and expanding mental life and not only occasion but demand reconstruction of mental attitudes. What is striking about the Hindu social order is its ban on free inter-change and intercourse between different classes of Hindu society. There is a bar against inter-dining and inter-marriage. But Manu goes to the length of interdicting ordinary social intercourse. Says Manu,

> IV. 244. 'He, who seeks to preserve an exalted rank, must constantly form connections with the highest and best families, but avoid the worst and the meanest'.
> IV. 245. 'Since a priest, who connects himself with the best and the highest of men, avoiding the lowest and worst, attains eminence; but sinks by an opposite conduct, to the class of the servile'.
> IV. 79. 'Not let him tarry even under the shade of the same tree with outcaste for the great crimes, nor with Chandalas, nor with Puccasas, nor with idiots, nor with man proud of wealth, nor with washermen and other vile persons, nor with Antyevasins'.

The Hindu social order is opposed to fraternity. It does not admit the principle of equality. Far from recognising equality it makes inequality its official doctrine. What about liberty? So far as choice of occupation goes, there is none. Everyone has his occupation determined for him. Only thing left to do is to carry it on. As to freedom of speech it exists. But it exists only for those who are in favour of the social order. The freedom is not the freedom of liberalism which was expressed by Voltaire when he said, 'I wholly disapprove of what you say and will defend to the death your right to say it'. This is clear from what Manu has to say about Logic and dialectics.

IV. 29-30. 'No guest must stay in his house without being honoured according to his ability, with a seat, food, a couch, water, or roots and fruits'.

Let him not honour even by a greeting heretics, men who follow forbidden occupations, men who live like cats, rogues, logicians (arguing against the Veda) and those who live like herons.

II. 10. 'But by Sruti (Revelation) is meant the Vedas and by Smriti (tradition) the Institutes of the sacred law; those two must not be called into question in any matter, since from those two the sacred law shone forth'.
II. 11. 'Every twice-born man, who, relying on the Institutes of dialectics, treats with contempt those two sources (of the law), must be cast out by the virtuous as an atheist and a scorner of the Veda'.
II. 12. 'The Veda, the sacred tradition, the customs of virtuous men, and one's own pleasure, they declare to be visibly the fourfold means of defining the sacred law'.

The reasons for this are made manifest by Manu who says,

II. 6. 'The whole Veda is the (first) source of the sacred law, next the tradition and the virtuous conduct of those who know the (Veda further) also the customs of holy men, and (finally) self-satisfaction'.
II. 7. Whatever law has been ordained for any (person) by Manu; that has been fully declared in the Veda; for that (sage was) omniscient'.

In this freedom there is not freedom for dialecticians, no freedom for logicians to criticise the social order which means there is no freedom at all.

What about liberty of action? In the sense of effective choice, there is no room for it in the Hindu social order. The Hindu social order leaves no choice to the individual. It fixes his occupation.

It fixes his status. All that remains for the individual to do is to conform himself to these regulations.

The same must be said with regard to political liberty. The Hindu social order does not recognise the necessity of a representative government composed of the representatives chosen by the people. Representative Government rests on the belief that people must be governed by law and law can be made only by the representative of the people. The Hindu social order recognises the first part of this thesis which says that people must be governed by law. But it denies the second part of the thesis which says that law can be made only by the representatives chosen by the people. The tenets of the Hindu social order is that the law by which people are to be governed is already made and is to be found in the Vedas. Nobody has a right to add to and subtract from it. That being so, a representative assembly of the people is unnecessary. Political liberty which is liberty to frame laws and to make and unmake Government is futility for which there is no place in the Hindu social order.

To sum up, the Hindu social order is an order based on classes and not on individual. It is an order in which classes are graded one above the other. It is an order in which the status and functions of the classes are determined and fixed. The Hindu social order is a rigid order. No matter what changes take place in the relative position of an individual his social status as a member of the class he is born in relation to another person belonging to another class shall in no way be affected. The first shall never become the last. The last shall never become the first.

CHAPTER 5

THE HINDU SOCIAL ORDER: ITS UNIQUE FEATURES

So far the discussions were confined to describing the essentials of the Hindu social order. Besides its essentials, the Hindu social order has some unique features. These unique features are as important as the essentials. No study of the Hindu social order which does not make any reference to them can be regraded as complete or accurate.

What are these special features? The special features of the Hindu social order are three in number. Of these three, the most striking is the worship of the superman. In this respect the Hindu social order is nothing but Nietzsche's Gospel put in action. Nietzsche himself never claimed any originality for his theory of the superman. He admitted and avowed that he borrowed it from the *Manu Smriti*. In his treatise, called *Anti-Christ* this is what Nietzsche said,

> After all, the question is, to what end are falsehoods perpetrated? The fact that, in Christianity, 'Holy' ends are entirely absent, constitutes

my objection to the means it employs. Its ends are only bad ends; the poisoning, the calumination and the denial of life, the contempt of the body, the degradation and self-pollution of man by virtue of the contempt of sin, – consequently its means are bad as well. My feelings are quite the reverse when I read the law book of Manu, an incomparably intellectual and superior work, which it would be a sin against the spirit even to mention in the same breath with the Bible. You will guess immediately why it has a genuine philosophy behind it. In it, not merely an evil smelling Jewish distillation of Rabbinism and superstition – it gives something to chew even to the most fastidious psychologist. And, not to forget the most important point of all, it is fundamentally different from the very kind of Bible; by means of it the noble classes, the philosophers and the warriors guard and guide the masses; it is replete with noble values, it is filled with a feeling of perfection with saying yea to life, triumphant sense of well-being in regard to itself and to life, – the Sun shines upon the whole book. All those things which Christianity smothers with its bottomless vulgarity; procreation, women, marriage are here treated with earnestness, with reverence, with love and confidence. How can one possibly place in the hands of children and women, a book that contains those vile words;' to avoid fornication let every man have his wife, let every woman have her own husband . . . It is better to marry than to burn. And is it decent to be a Christian so long as the very origin of man is Christianised – that is to say, befouled, by the idea of the immaculate conception.[1]

Nietzsche never got any respectful or serious hearing in his own country. In his own words, he was 'sometimes defied as the philosopher of the aristocracy and squiarchy, sometimes hooted

[1] [*Editor's Note*: Friedrich Nietzsche's *The Anti-Christ* was published in 1895. It was a direct assault on Christianity and Judaism, both of which Nietzsche associated with the 'decadence of modernity'. The book had been completed by 1888, but Nietzsche's publisher held up its release for fear of its contents.]

at, sometimes pitied and sometimes boycotted as an inhuman being'. Nietzsche's philosophy had become identified with *will to power*, will to violence and denial of spiritual values, sacrifice, servility to and debasement of the common man in the interest of the Superman. His philosophy with these high spots had created a feeling of loathsomeness and horror in the minds of the people of his own generation. He was utterly neglected if not shunned and Nietzsche himself took comfort by placing himself among the 'posthumous men'. He foresaw for himself a remote public, centuries after his own time to appreciate him. Here too Nietzsche was destined to be disappointed. Instead of there being any appreciation of his philosophy the lapse of time has only augmented the horror and loathing which people of his generation felt for Nietzsche. Having regard to the vile nature of Nietzsche's philosophy some people may not be ready to believe that the Hindu social order is based on the worship of the Superman.

Let the Manu Smriti speak on this point. This is what Manu says with regard to the position of the Brahman in the Hindu social order.

> I. 93. 'As the Brahmana sprang from Prajapati's (i.e. God's) mouth, as he was first-born, and as he possesses the Veda, he is by right the Lord of this whole creation'.
>
> I. 94. 'For the self-existent (Swayambhu) i.e. God having performed austerities, produced him first from his own mouth, in order that the offerings might be conveyed to the Gods and Manes and that this universe might be preserved'.
>
> I. 95. 'What created being can surpass him, through whose mouth the Gods continually consume the sacrificial viands and the Manes the offerings to the dead'.
>
> I. 96. 'Of created beings the most excellent are said to be those which are animated, of the animated those who subsist by intelligence; of

the intelligent mankind, and of the men the Brahmans'.

Besides the reason given by Manu, the Brahman is first in rank because he was produced by God from his mouth, in order that the offerings might be conveyed to the Gods and manes, Manu gives another reason for the supremacy of the Brahman. He says,

> I. 98. 'The very birth of a Brahmana is an eternal incarnation of the sacred law (Veda) for he is born to (fulfil) the sacred law, and becomes one with Brahman (God.)'.
> I. 99. 'A Brahmana coming into existence, is born as the highest on earth, the Lord of all created beings, for the protection of the treasury of the law'.

Manu concludes by saying that,

> I. 101. 'The Brahmana eats but his own food, wears but his own apparel, bestows but his own in alms; other mortals subsist through the benevolence of the Brahmana'.

Because according to Manu,

> I. 100. 'Whatever exists in the world is the property of the Brahmana; on account of the excellence of his origin the Brahmana is, indeed, entitled to it all'

Being a deity the Brahman is above law and above the king. Manu directs,

> VII. 37. 'Let the king, rising early in the morning, worship Brahmanas who are well-versed in the threefold sacred science and learned (in polity) and follow their advice'.

VII. 38. 'Let him daily worship aged Brahmans who know the Veda and are pure'.

Finally Manu says,

XI. 35. 'The Brahman is (hereby) declared to be the creator (of the world), the punisher, the teacher, (and hence) a benefactor (of all created beings) to him let no man say anything unpropitious, nor use any harsh words'.

Manu ordains that,

X. 3. 'From priority of birth, from superiority of origin, from a more exact knowledge of scripture, and from a distinction in the sacrificial thread, the Brahman is the lord of all classes'.

The Brahman or the Superman of the Hindu social order was entitled to certain privileges. In the first place, he could not be hanged even though he might be guilty of murder.[2] Manu says,

VIII. 379. 'Ignominous tonsure is ordained, instead of capital punishment, for a Brahman adulterer where the punishment of other classes may extend to loss of life'.

VIII. 380. 'Never shall the king slay a Brahman, though convicted of all possible crimes; let him banish the offender from his realm, but with all his property secure, and his body unhurt'.

XI. 127. 'For a Brahman killing intentionally a virtuous man of the

[2] This immunity was continued by the British Government up to 1837. It was in 1837 the Penal Law was amended whereby the Brahman for the first time became liable to capital punishment for murder. The immunity still exists in Indian States. In Travancore the Dewan who is a Brahman adopted an ingenious method of meeting public criticism of this continuance of this privilege, instead of hanging the Brahmans he abolished capital punishment altogether.

Kshatriya class, the penance must be a fourth part of that ordained for killing a priest; for killing a Vaishya, only an eighth; for killing a Shudra, who had been constant in discharging his duties a sixteenth part'.

XI. 128. 'But, if a Brahman kills a Kshatriya without malice, he must, after a full performance of his religious rites, give the priests one bull together with a thousand cows'.

XI. 129. 'Or he may perform for three years the penance for slaying a Brahman, mortifying his organs of sensation and action, letting his hair grow long, and living remote from the town, with the root of a tree for his mansion'.

XI. 130. 'If he kills without malice a Vaishya, who had a good moral character, he may perform the same penance for one year, or give the priests a hundred cows and a bull'.

XI. 131. 'For six months must, he perform this whole penance, if without intention he kills a Shudra, or he may give ten white cows and a bull to the priests'.

VIII. 381. 'No greater crime is known on earth than slaying a Brahman; and the king, therefore must not even form in his mind an idea of killing a priest'.

VIII. 126. 'Let the king having considered and ascertained the frequency of a similar offence, the place and time, the ability of the criminal to pay or suffer and the crime itself, cause punishment to fall on those alone, who deserve it'.

VIII. 124. 'Manu, son of the self-existent, has named ten places of punishment, which are appropriated to the three lower classes, but a Brahman must depart from the realm unhurt in any one of them'.

The Brahman has been given by the *Manu Smriti* other privileges. In the matter of marriage in addition to his marrying a woman of his own class he is entitled[3] to enter into wedlock with a

[3] Manu III. 12-13. This privilege is recognised by Courts in India.

woman of any of the classes lower to him without being bound to the woman by the tie of marriage or conferring upon the children the right to his status or to his property. He had the power to punish his wrongdoer without resort to court.[4] He could take the property of the common man (the Shudra) without compensation and without reference to court if the same was necessary for the performance of his religious duties.[5] If he discovers a hidden treasure he was free to appropriate the whole[6] of it without giving the usual share to the king 'since he was the lord of all' and was entitled to claim half[7] if it was discovered by another. He was entitled to the whole amount accumulated from legal fines from a king whose death was due to some incurable disease.[8] He was exempt from taxation.[9] He was entitled to compel the king to provide for his daily food and to see that he did not starve.[10] His property was free from the law of escheat.[11] The superman of the Hindu social order is not bound by the rules as to occupation if he is in distress.

Manu says,

> X. 81. 'Yet a Brahman, unable to subsist by his duties just mentioned, may live by the duty of a soldier; for that is the next in rank'.
> X. 82. 'If it be asked, how he must live, should he be unable to get a subsistence by either of those employments; the answer is, he may subsist as a mercantile man, applying himself in person to tillage and attendance on cattle'.

[4] Manu XI. 31 – This privilege has been abolished.
[5] Manu XI. 32 – This privilege no longer exists.
[6] Manu VIII. 37.
[7] Manu VIII. 38.
[8] Manu IX. 323.
[9] Manu VII. 133.
[10] Manu VII. 134.
[11] Manu IX. 189.

X. 83. 'But a Brahman and a Kshatriya, obliged to subsist by the acts of a Vaishya, must avoid with care, if they can live by keeping herds, the business of tillage, which gives great pain to sentient creatures, and is dependent on the labour of others, as bulls and so forth'.

X. 84. 'Some are of opinion, that agriculture is excellent but it is a mode of subsistence which the benevolent greatly blame, for the iron mouthed pieces of wood not only wound the earth, but the creatures dwelling in it'.

X. 85. 'If, through want of a virtuous livelihood, they cannot follow laudable occupations, they may then gain a competence of wealth by selling commodities usually sold by merchants, avoiding what ought to be avoided'.

X. 102. 'The Brahmana, having fallen into distress, may receive gifts from any person whatever; for by no sacred rule can it be shown, that absolute purity can be sullied'.

X. 103. 'From interpreting the Veda, from officiating at sacrifices or from taking presents, though in modes generally disapproved, no sin is committed by priests in distress; for they are as pure as fire or water'.

The privileges of the Superman are not at all counterbalanced by an obligation towards the Common man. Indeed the Superman has no duty towards the Common man.

He is not bound to do charity for the uplift of the Common man. On the other hand, to receive charity is the monopoly of the Superman. For any other person to receive charity is a sin. To the Common man (Shudra) who is born to serve the Superman, the Superman is not at all required to be a good employer and is not bound to keep him well-fed, well-clothed and well-housed. His obligations in this behalf as laid down by Manu are stated below,

X. 124. 'They must allot to him (Shudra) out of their own family property a suitable maintenance after considering his ability, his industry and the number of those whom he is bound to support'.

X. 125. 'The remnants of their food must be given to him, as well as their old clothes, the refuse of their grain, and their old household furniture'.

The rise of the Common man is antagonistic to the supremacy of the Superman. In order to keep the Superman satisfied, happy and secure the Hindu social order takes special care to keep the Common man in a state of perpetual degradation. Manu insists on the Shudra doing nothing but service,

X. 122. 'But let a Shudra serve Brahmanas'.

X. 121. 'If a Shudra unable to subsist by serving Brahmanas seeks a livelihood, he may serve Kshatriyas, or he may also seek to maintain himself by attending on a wealthy Vaishya'.

I. 91. 'One occupation only the lord prescribed to the Shudra, to serve meekly even these other three castes'.

And why? Manu does not hesitate to give the reason. He says,

X. 129. 'No superfluous collection of wealth must be made by a Shudra, even though he has power to make it, since a servile man, who has amassed riches, becomes proud, and, by his insolence or neglect, gives pain even to Brahmanas'.

The Common man is not permitted to acquire learning. The following are the injunctions of Manu.

I. 88. 'To the Brahmanas he (the creator) assigned teaching and studying the Veda'.

I. 89. 'The Kshatriya he (the creator) commanded to study the Veda'.

> II. 116. 'He who shall acquire knowledge of the Veda without the assent of his preceptor incurs the guilt of stealing the scripture, and shall sink to the region of torment'.
> IV. 99. 'He (the twice-born) must never read the Veda . . . in the presence of the Shudras'.
> IX. 18. 'Women have no business with the text of the Veda'.
> IX. 199. 'A twice-born man who has (improperly) divulged the Veda (i.e., to Shudras and women) commits sin, atones for his offence, if he subsists a year on barley'.

In those texts there are embodied three distinct propositions. The Brahmans, Kshatriyas and Vaishyas can study the Vedas. Of these the Brahmans alone have the right to teach the Vedas. But in the case of the Shudra he has not only to not study the Vedas but he should not be allowed to hear it read.

The successors of Manu made the disability of the Shudra in the matter of the study of the Veda into an offence involving dire penalties. For instance, Gautama says,

> III. 4. 'If the Shudra intentionally listens for committing to memory the Veda, then his ears should be filled with (molten) lead and lac; if he utters the Veda, then his tongue should be cut off; if he has mastered the Veda his body should be cut to pieces'.

To the same effect is Katyayana.

The Common man (Shudra) is not allowed the benefit of the sacrament of initiation. It is the second birth that helps towards the moral and material advancement of the individual.

The Common man is denied the right to have a name conveying dignity. Manu says,

> II. 30. 'Let the father perform or cause to be performed the

Namadheya (the rite of name of the child), on the tenth or twelfth (day after birth), or on a lucky lunar day in a lucky muhurth under an auspicious constellation'.

II. 31. 'Let (the first part of) a Brahman's name (denote something) auspicious, a Kshatriya name be connected with power, and a Vaishya with wealth, but a Shudra's (express something) contemptible'.

II. 32. '(The second part of) a Brahman's name shall be a word implying happiness, of a Kshatriya (a word) implying protection, of a Vaishya (a term) expressive of thriving and of a Shudra's (an expression) denoting a service'.

The Superman will not tolerate the Shudra to have the comfort of a high-sounding name. He must be contemptible both in fact and in name.

A Hindu's life is divided into periods. The first period is called Brahmacharya, the stage of a student. The second period is called Grahasthashram, the stage of married life. The third period is called Vanasprastha, the stage of detachment from worldly life. The fourth period is called Sanyasa which is complete severance from the affairs of the world which is tantamount to civil death. The common man is denied the right of becoming a Sanyasi. It is difficult to understand why. Obviously for the benefit of the Superman. A Shudra by becoming a Sanyasi ceases to render service to the Superman. A Shudra by becoming a Sanyasi reaches God or Brahma which is an invasion of the privileges of the Superman.

The citations from Manu prove that the Hindu social order is openly and avowedly devised and intended for the good of the Superman. In it everything is ordained for the Superman. The Superman is the Brahman and the Common man is the Shudra. The Superman has rights and no duties. Everything is at the disposal of the Superman, everything must be ascribed in the interests of the

Superman. The counterpart of the same feature is the degradation of the Common man. As against the Superman the Common man has no right to life, liberty, property or pursuit of happiness. He must be ready to sacrifice everything for the sustenance of the life and dignity of the Superman. The Hindu social order prescribes that such sacrifice should be made willingly by the Common man. Indeed, it inculcates that the Common man should respond to such call for sacrifice in the interest of the Superman as his supreme duty.

Can there be any doubt that Zarathustra is a new name for Manu and that *Thus Spake Zarathustra*[12] is a new edition of the *Manu Smriti*?

If there is any difference between Manu and Nietzsche, it lies in this. Nietzsche was genuinely interested in creating a new race of men which will be a race of Superman as compared with the existing race of men. Manu, on the other hand, was interested in maintaining the privilege of a class who had come to arrogate to itself the claim of being Superman. Nietzsche's Supermen were Supermen by reason of their worth. Nietzsche was a genuine distinterested philosopher. Manu, on the contrary, was a hireling engaged to propound a philosophy which served the interests of a class, born in a group and whose title to being Superman was not to be lost even if they lost their virtue. Compare the following texts from Manu,[13]

[12] [*Editor's Note*: *Thus Spake Zarathustra* was written by Friedrich Nietzsche between 1883 and 1885. It was published between 1883 and 1891. The main theme here was the journey of the *Übermensch*, the Over Man or Superman, from the mere position of Man – a step above Animal but still beneath the heights it is capable of ascending. There is a debate over whether Nietzsche meant that the Superman was a different race or whether this was a book about self-mastery of humankind in general.]

[13] The correct description of the Brahman would be the Supermost Superman. For below him and above the common man there are the Kshatriyas and the Vaishyas. But since the Kshatriyas and the Vaishyas are only superiors and not supermen it is unnecessary to change the nomenclature.

> X. 81. 'Yet, a Brahman, unable to subsist by his duties just mentioned, may live by the duty of a soldier; for that is the next rank'.
> X. 82. 'If it be asked, how he must live, should he be unable to get a subsistence by either of those employments; the answer is, he may subsist as a mercantile man, applying himself to tillage and an attendance on cattle'.

Manu adds,

> IX. 317. 'A Brahman, be he ignorant or learned, is a great divinity, just as the fire, whether carried forth (for the performance of a burnt oblation) or not carried forth, is a great divinity'.
> IX. 319. 'Thus, though the Brahmans employ themselves in all (sorts) of mean occupation, they must be honoured in every way; (for each of) them is a very great deity'.

Nietzsche's praise of the Manu Smriti is undeserved. For when he says that according to its scheme 'the noble classes, the philosophers and the warriors guard and guide the masses', he is either making a positively untrue statement or that he has not read it correctly. Under the *Manu Smriti* the Superman has rights against the Common man but he has no duties towards the Common man.

Manu's degraded and degenerate philosophy of Superman as compared with that of Nietzsche is therefore far more odious and loathsome than the philosophy of Nietzsche. Such is the social order which the Hindus regard as a pearl without price and which Mr. Gandhi is proud to offer as a gift from the Hindus to the world.

Another special feature of the Hindu social order relates to the technique devised for its preservation. The technique is twofold.

The first technique is to place the responsibility of upholding and maintaining the social order upon the shoulders of the King. Manu does this in quite express terms.

VIII. 410. 'The King should order each man of the mercantile class to practise trade or money-lending or agriculture and attendance on cattle; and each man of the servile class to act in the service of the twice-born'.

VIII. 418. 'With vigilant care should the King exert himself in compelling merchants and mechanics to perform their respective duties; for, when such men swerve from their duty they throw this world into confusion'.

Manu does not stop with the mere enunciation of the duty of the King in this behalf. He wants to ensure that the King shall at all times perform his duty to maintain and preserve the established order. Manu therefore makes two further provisions. One provision is to make the failure of the King to maintain the established order an offence for which the King became liable for prosecution and punishment like a common felon. This would be clear from the following citations from Manu,

VIII. 335. 'Neither a father, nor a preceptor, nor a friend, nor a mother, nor a wife, nor a son, nor a domestic priest must be left unpunished by the King if they adhere not with firmness to their duty'.

VIII. 336. 'Where another man of lower birth would be fined one pana, the King shall be fined a thousand, and he shall give the fine to the priests, or cast it into the river, this is a sacred rule'.

The other provision made by Manu against a King who is either negligent or opposed to the established order is to invest the three classes, Brahmans, Kshatriyas and Vaishyas with a right to rise in armed rebellion against the King.

VIII. 348. 'The twice-born may take arms, when their duty is obstructed by force; and when, in some evil time, a disaster has befallen the twice-born classes'.

The right of rebellion is given to the three higher classes and not to the Shudra. This is very natural. Because it is only the three upper classes who would benefit by the maintenance of this system. But supposing the Kshatriyas joined the king in destroying the system what is to be done? Manu gives the authority to the Brahmans to punish all and particularly the Kshatriyas.

XI. 31. 'A priest, who well knows the laws, need not complain to the king of any grievous injury; since, even by his own power, he may chastise those, who injure him'.
XI. 32. 'His own power, which depends on himself alone, is mightier than the royal power, which depends on other men; by his own might, therefore, may a Brahman coerce his foes'.
XI. 33. 'He may use, without hesitation, the powerful charms revealed to Atharvan, and by him to Angiras; for speech is the weapon of a Brahman; with that he may destroy his oppressors'.
IX. 320. 'Of a military man, who raises his arm violently on all occasions against the priestly class, the priest himself shall be the chastiser; since the soldier originally proceeded from the Brahman'.

How can the Brahmans punish the Kshatriyas unless they can take arms? Manu knows this and therefore allows the Brahmans to arm themselves to punish the Kshatriyas.

XII. 100. 'Command of armies, royal authority, power of inflicting punishment, and sovereign dominion over all nations, he only well deserves, who perfectly understands the Veda Sastra i.e., who is a Brahman'.

The second technique devised for the maintenance and preservation of the established order is quite different from the first. Really speaking, it is this which constitutes a special feature of the Hindu social order.

In the wake of the preservation of the social order from violent attack it is necessary to bear in mind three considerations. The outbreak of a revolution is conditioned by three factors: (1) the existence of a sense of wrong; (2) capacity to know that one is suffering from a wrong and (3) availability of arms. The second consideration is that there are two ways of dealing with a rebellion. One is to prevent a rebellion from occurring and the other is to suppress it after it has broken out. The third consideration is that whether the prevention of rebellion would be feasible or whether the suppression of rebellion would be the only method open, would depend upon the rules which govern the three pre-requisites of rebellion.

When the social order denies opportunity to rise, denies right to education and denies right to use arms, it is in a position to prevent rebellion against the social order. Where on the other hand, a social order allows right to education, and permits the use of arms, it cannot prevent rebellion by those who suffer wrongs. Its only remedy to preserve the social order is by suppression of rebellion by the use of force and violence. The Hindu social order has adopted the first method. It has fixed the social status of the lower orders for all generations to come. Their economic status is also fixed. There being no disparity between the two, there is no possibility of a grievance growing up. It has denied education to the lower orders. The result is that no one is conscious that his low condition is a ground for grievance. If there is any consciousness it is that no one is responsible for the low condition. It is the result of fate. Assuming there is a grievance, assuming there is consciousness of grievance, there cannot be a rebellion by the lower orders against the Hindu social order because the Hindu social order denies the masses the right to use arms. Other social orders such as those of the Muslims or the Nazis, follow the opposite course. They allow equal opportunity to all. They allow freedom to acquire knowledge. They allow the right to bear arms and take upon themselves the odium of suppressing rebellion by force and violence. To deny freedom of opportunity, to deny freedom to acquire knowledge, to deny the right of arms is a most cruel wrong. Its results Manu mutilates and emasculates man. The Hindu social order is not ashamed to do this. It has, however, achieved two things. It has found the most effective, even though it be the most shameless method of preserving the established order. Secondly, notwithstanding the use of most inhuman means of killing manliness, it has given to the Hindus the reputation of being very humane people. The Nazis had indeed a great deal to learn from the Hindus. If they had adopted the technique of suppressing the masses devised by the Hindus they would have been able to crush the Jews without open cruelty and would have also exhibited themselves as humane masters.

The third special feature of the Hindu social order is that it is a Divine order designed by God himself. As such it is sacred, not open to abrogation, amendment, not even to criticism. For the purpose of removing any doubt that may be lurking in the minds of anybody about the Divine character of the Hindu social order, attention is invited to the following verses from the *Bhagavat Gita* and the *Manu Smriti*. Shri Krishna one of the Hindu Gods, whose word is the *Bhagavat Gita* says,

> IV. 13. 'I myself have created the arrangement of the four castes (into Brahmans, Kshatriyas, Vaishyas and Shudras), consistently with the differences in their qualities and actions. It is I who am the Maker of it'.

> XVIII. 41-44. 'O, Parantapa! the respective duties of Brahmans (priests), Kshatriyas (warriors), Vaishyas (tradesmen) and Shudras (menials) have been individually fixed with reference to the qualities arising from their inherent natures, that is, from Prakriti. The inherently natural duties of a Brahman are peace, self-restrain, religious austerities, cleanliness, quietness, straightforwardness (humanity). Knowledge (that is, spiritual knowledge), Vijnana (that is Imperial knowledge) and Astikya-budhi (that is belief in a future world). The inherently natural duty (karma) of the Kshatriya is bravery, brilliance, courage, intentness, not running away from the battle, generosity, and exercising authority (over subject people) 'goraksya' (that is the business of keeping cattle), and vanijya (that is, trade) is the inherently natural duty of the Vaishya; and in the same way, service is the inherently natural duty of the Shudra'.

Krishna forbids propaganda against the Hindu social order. He says,

> III. 26. 'As the ignorant act with attachment to action so a wise man wishing to keep the people to their duties, should not shake the convictions of the ignorant who are attached to action, but acting with devotion (himself) should make them apply themselves to all action . . . . A man of perfect knowledge should not shake these men of imperfect knowledge in their convictions'.

When the Hindu social order breaks down, Krishna does not want the people to undertake the work of reform. He asks them to leave the task to him. This is evident from the following admonition contained in the *Bhagavat Gita*. Says Krishna,

> IV. 7-8. 'O! Bharata, whenever Righteousness declines and Unrighteousness becomes powerful, then I Myself come to birth.

I take birth in different Yugas for protecting the Righteous and destroying the Unrighteous and for establishing Righteousness'.

It is not only a special feature of the Hindu social order. It is an extraordinary feature. An examination of consecrations will show that there are instances where society has consecrated inanimate beings and inculcated on the minds of its members the religious belief that they are sacred. There are cases where stones, rivers, trees are made Gods and Goddesses. There are instances where society has consecrated living things and inculcated on the minds of its members the religious belief that they are sacred. But there are no instances where a particular social order has been consecrated by religion and made sacred. The primitive world had its clan order and its tribal order. But the clan or the tribal order was only a social order and was never consecrated by religion and made sacred and inviolate. The ancient world countries like Egypt, Persia, Rome, Greece, etc., each had its social order in which some were free and some were slaves, some were citizens, some were aliens, some of the race, some of another. This class order again was only a social order and was never consecrated by religion and made sacred and inviolate. The modern world has its order: in some it is Democracy, in some Fascism, in some Nazism and in some Bolshevism. But here again the order is only a social order. It is not consecrated by religion and made sacred and inviolate.

Nowhere this society consecrated its occupations – the ways of getting a living. Economic activity has always remained outside the sanctity of religion. Hunting society was not without religion. But Hunting as an occupation was not consecrated by religion and made sacred. Pastoral society was not without religion. But pasturage was not consecrated by religion and made sacred. Farming as an occupation did not become consecrated by religion and made sacred. Feudalism with its gradations, with its Lords, villains and serfs was a purely social in character. There was nothing sacred about it.

The Hindus are the only people in the world whose social order – the relation of man to man is consecrated by religion and made sacred, eternal and inviolate. The Hindus are the only people in the world whose economic order – the relation of workman to workman, is consecrated by religion and made sacred, eternal and inviolate.

It is not therefore enough to say that the Hindus are a people with a sacred code of religion. So are the Zoroastrians, Israelites, Christians and Muslims. All these have sacred codes. They consecrate beliefs and rites and make them sacred. But they do not prescribe, nor do they consecrate a particular form of social structure – the relationship between man and man in a concrete form – and make it sacred, inviolate. The Hindus are singular in this respect. This is what has given the Hindu social order its abiding strength to defy the ravages of time and the onslaught of time.

The orthodox Hindu will accept this as an accurate description of the Hindu social order. It is only the reformer who is likely to demur. He would say that since the advent of the British, this is all a description of a dead past. One need not be perturbed by this view. For it contains a fallacy. It omits to take note of the fact that institutions which have died as creeds sometimes continue, nevertheless to survive as habits. No one can deny that the Hindu social order has become the habit of the Hindus and as such is in full force.

ADDITIONAL SECTION

SYMBOLS OF HINDUISM

Is there anything peculiar in the social organization of the Hindus? An unsophisticated Hindu who is unaware of investigations conducted by scholars will say that there is nothing peculiar, abnormal or unnatural in the organisation of the Hindu society. This is quite natural. People who live their lives in isolation are seldom conscious of the peculiarities of their ways and manners. People have gone on from generation to generation without stopping to give themselves a name. But how does the social organisation of the Hindus strike the outsiders, the non-Hindus? Did it appear to them as normal and natural as it appears to the Hindus?

Megasthenes who came to India as the ambassador of the Greek King Seleukos Nickator to the Court of Chandragupta Maurya some time about the year 305 B.C. did feel that the social organisation of the Hindus was of a very strange sort. Otherwise, he would not have taken such particular care to describe the peculiar features of the Hindu social organisation. He has recorded,

> The population of India is divided into seven parts. The philosophers

are first in rank, but form the smallest class in point of number. Their services are employed privately by persons who wish to offer sacrifices or perform other sacred rites, and also publicly by the kings at what is called the Great Synod, wherein at the beginning of the new year all the philosophers are gathered together before the king at the gates, when any philosopher who may have committed any useful suggestion to writing, or observed any means for improving the crops and the cattle, or for promoting the public interests, declares it publicly. If anyone is detected giving false information thrice, the law condemns him to be silent for the rest of his life, but he who gives sound advice is exempted from paying any taxes or contributions.

The second caste consists of the husbandmen, who form the bulk of the population, and are in disposition most mild and gentle. They are exempted from military service, and cultivate their lands undisturbed by fear. They never go to town, either to take part in its tumults, or for any other purpose. It therefore not infrequently happens that at the same time, and in the same part of the country, men may be seen drawn up in array of battle, and fighting at risk of their lives, while other men close at hand are ploughing and digging in perfect security, having these soldiers to protect them. The whole of the land is the property of the king, and the husbandmen till it on condition of receiving one-fourth of the produce.

The third caste consists of herdsmen and hunters, who alone are allowed to hunt, and to keep cattle and to sell draught animals or let them out on hire. In return for clearing the land of wild beasts and fowls which devour the seeds sown in the fields, they receive an allowance of grain from the king. They lead a wandering life and live under tents.

The fourth class, after herdsmen and hunters, consists of those who work at trades, of those who vend wares, and of those who are employed in bodily labour. Some of these pay tribute, and render to the state certain prescribed services. But the armour makers and shipbuilders receive wages and their victuals from the king, for whom alone they work. The general in command of the army supplies the soldiers with weapons, and the admiral of the fleet lets out ships on hire for the transport both of passengers and merchandise.

The fifth class consists of fighting men, who when not engaged in active service, pass their time in idleness and drinking. They are maintained at the king's expense, and hence they are always ready, when occasion calls, to take the field, for they carry nothing of their own with them but their own bodies.

The sixth class consists of the overseers, to whom is assigned the duty of watching all that goes on, and making reports secretly to the king. Some are entrusted with the inspection of the city, and others with that of the army. The former employ as their coadjutors the courtesans of the city, and the latter the courtesans of the camp. The ablest and most trustworthy men are appointed to fill these offices.

The seventh class consists of the Councilors and assessors of the king. To them belong the highest posts of government, the tribunals of justice, and the general administration of public affairs. No one is allowed to marry out of his own caste, or to exchange one profession or trade for another, or to follow more than one business. An exception is made in favour of the philosopher, who for his virtue is allowed this privilege.

Alberuni who wrote an account of his travels in India some time about 1030 A.D. must have been struck by the peculiarity of the Hindu social organization. For he too has not omitted to make a note of it in the record of impressions he made. He observed,

The Hindus call their castes varna i.e. colours, and from a genealogical point of view they call them jataka i. e., births. These castes are from the very beginning only four.

1. The highest caste are the Brahmans of whom the books of the

Hindus tell that they were created from the head of Brahma. And a Brahma is only another name for the force called nature, and the head is the highest part of the animal body, the Brahmana are the choice part of the whole genus. Therefore the Hindus consider them as the very best of mankind.

2. The next caste are the Kshatriyas, who were created, as they say, from the shoulders and hands of Brahma. Their degree is not much below that of the Brahmana.
3. After them follow the Vaisyas, who were created from the thigh of Brahma.
4. The Sudras, who were created from his feet.

Between the latter two classes there is no very great distance. Much, however, as these classes differ from each other, they live together in the same towns and villages, mixed together in the same houses and lodgings.

After the Sudra follow the people called Antyaja, who render various kinds of services, who are not reckoned amongst any caste, but only as members of a certain craft or profession. There are eight classes of them who freely intermarry with each other, except the fuller, shoemaker and weaver, for no others would condescend to have anything to do with them. These eight guilds are the fuller, shoemaker, juggler, the basket and shield maker, the sailor, fisherman, the hunter of wild animals and of birds, and the weaver. The four castes do not live together with them in one and the same place. These guilds live near the villages and towns of the four castes, but outside them.

The people called Hadi, Doma (Domba), Candala, and Badhatau (sic) are not reckoned amongst any caste or guild. They are occupied with dirty work, like the cleansing of the villages and other services. They are considered as one sole class, and distinguished only by their occupations. In fact, they are considered like illegitimate children; for according to general opinion they descend from a Sudra father and a Brahmani mother as the children of fornication; therefore they are degraded outcaste.

The Hindus give to every single man of the four castes characteristic names, according to their occupations and modes of life, eg., the Brahman is in general called by this name as long as he does his work staying at home. When he is busy with the service of one fire, he is called *Ishtin*; if he serves three fires, he is called *Agnihotrin*; if he besides offers an offering to the fire, he is called *Dikshita*. And as it is with the Brahmana, so is it also with the other castes. Of the classes beneath the castes, the Hadi are the best spoken of, because they keep themselves free from everything unclean. Next follow the Doma, who play on the lute and sing. The still lower classes practise as a trade killing and the inflicting of judicial punishments. The worst of all are the Badhantan, who not only devour the flesh of dead animals, but even of dogs and other beasts.

Each of the four castes, when eating together, must form a group of themselves, one group not being allowed to comprise two men of different castes. If, further, in the group of the Brahman there are two men who live at enmity with each other, and the seat of the one is by the side of the other, they make a barrier between the two seats by placing a board between them, or by spreading a piece of dress, or in some other way; and if there is only a line drawn between them, they are considered as separated. Since it is forbidden to eat the remains of a meal, every single man must have his own food for himself, for if anyone of the party who are eating should take of the food from one and the same plate, that which remains in the plate becomes, after the first eater has taken part, to him who wants to take as the second, the remains of the meal as such is forbidden.

Alberuni did not merely content himself with recording what struck him as peculiar in the Hindu social organization. He went on to say,

> Among the Hindus institutions of this kind abound. We Muslims, of course, stand entirely on the other side of the question, considering all men as equal, except in piety; and this is the greatest obstacle which prevents any approach or understanding between Hindus and Muslims.

Duarte Barbosa who was a Portuguese official in the service of the Portuguese Government in India from 1500 to 1571 has left a record of his impressions of Hindu society. This is what struck him in speaking of the kingdom of Gujarat,

> And before this kingdom Guzerate fell into the hands of the Moors. A certain caste of Heathen whom the Moors called Resbutos (Rajputs) dwelt therein, who in those days were the knights and wardens of the land, and made war wheresoever it was needful. These men kill and eat sheep and fish and all other kinds of food; in the mountains there are yet many of the them, where they have great villages and obey not the king of Guzarate, but rather wage daily war against him; who, do what he may, is yet not able to prevail against them, nor will do so, for they are very fine horsemen, and good archers, and have besides divers other weapons to defend themselves withal against the Moors, on whom they make war without ceasing; yet have they no king nor lord over them. And in this kingdom there is another sort of Heathen whom they call Baneanes, who are great merchants and traders. They dwell among the Moors with whom they carry on all their trade. This people eat neither flesh nor fish nor anything subject to death; they slay nothing, nor are they willing even to see the slaughter of any animal; and thus they maintain their idolatry and hold it so firmly that it is a terrible thing. For often it is so that the Moors take to them live insects or small birds, and make as though to kill them in their presence, and the Baneanes buy these and ransom them, paying much more than they are worth,

so that they may save their lives and let them go. And if the King or a Governor of the land has any man condemned to death, for any crime which he has committed, they gather themselves together and buy him from justice, if they are willing to sell him, that he may not die. And divers Moorish mendicants as well, when they wish to obtain alms from this people, take great stones wherewith they beat upon their shoulders and bellies as though they would slay themselves before them, to hinder which they give them great alms that they may depart in peace. Others carry knives with which they slash their arms and legs, and to these too they give large alms that they may not kill themselves. Others go to their doors seeking to kill rats and snakes for them, and to them also they give much money that they may not do so. Thus they are much esteemed by the Moors. When these Baneanes meet with a swarm of ants on the road they shrink back and seek for some way to pass without crushing them. And in their houses they sup by daylight, for neither by night nor by day will they light a lamp, by reason of certain little flies which perish in the flame thereof; and if there is any great need of a light by night they have a lantern of varnished paper or cloth, so that no living thing may find its way in, and die in the flame. And if these men breed many lice they kill them not, but when they trouble them too much they send for certain men, also Heathen, who living among them and whom they hold to be men of a holy life, they are like hermits living with great abstinence through devotion to their gods. These men house them, and as many lice as they catch they place on their own heads and breed them on their own flesh, by which they say they do great service to their Idol. Thus one and all they maintain with great self-restraint their law of not killing. On the other hand they are great usurers, falsifiers of weights and measures and many other goods and of coins; and great liars. These Heathen are tawny men, tail and well-looking gaily attired, delicate and moderate in their food. Their diet is of milk, butter, sugar and rice, and many conserves of divers sorts. They make much use of dishes of fruit and vegetables and pot herbs in their food. Wheresoever they dwell they have orchards and fruit gardens and many water tanks wherein they bathe twice a day, both men and women; and they say when they have finished bathing that they are clear of as many sins as they have committed up to that hour. These Baneanes grow very long hair, as women do with us, and wear it twisted up on the head and made into a knot, and over it a turban, that they may keep it always held together; and in their hair they put flowers and other sweet scented things.

They use to anoint themselves with white sandalwood mixed with saffron and other scents. They are very amorous people. They are clad in long cotton and silken shirts and are shod with pointed shoes of richly wrought cordwain; some of them wear short coats of silk and brocade. They carry no arms except certain very small knives ornamented with gold and silver, and this for two reasons; first because they are men who make but little use of weapons; and secondly, because the Moors defend them.

And there is here another class of Heathen whom they call Brahmenes, who are priests among them and persons who manage and rule their houses of prayer and idol-worship, which are of great size and have great revenues; and many of them also are maintained by alms. In these houses are great numbers of wooden Idols, and others of stone and copper and in these houses or monasteries they celebrate great ceremonies in honour of these idols, entertaining them with great store of candles and oil lamps, and with bells after our fashion. These Brahmenes and Heathen have in their creed many resemblances to the Holy Trinity, and hold in great honour the relation of the Triune Three, and always make their prayers to God, whom they confess and adore as the true God, Creator and maker of all things, who is three persons and one God, and they say that there are many other Gods who are rulers under him, in whom also they believe. These Brahmenes and Heathen wheresoever they find our churches enter them and make prayers and adorations to our Images, always asking for Santa Maria, like men who have some knowledge and understanding of these matters and they honour the Church as is our manner, saying that between them and us there is little difference. These men never eat anything subject to death, nor do they slay anything. Bathing they hold to be a great ceremony and they say that by it they are saved.

Speaking of the Kingdom of Calicut, Barbosa says,

There is also in this same kingdom of Calicut a caste of people called Brahmenes who are priests among them (as are the clergy among us) of whom 1 have spoken in another place.

These all speak the same tongue, nor can any be a Brahmene except he be the son of a Brahmene. When they are seven years of age they put over their shoulder a strip of two fingers in breadth of untanned skin with the hair on it of a certain wild beast which they call Cryvamergam, which resembles a wild ass. Then for seven years he must not eat betel for which time he continues to wear this strap. When he is fourteen years old they make him a Brahmene, and taking off their leather strip they invest him with the cord of three strands which he wears for the rest of his life as a token that he is a Brahmene. And this they do with great ceremonial and rejoicings, as we do here for a cleric when he sings his first mass. Thereafter he may eat betel, but no flesh or fish. They have great honour among the Indians, and as I have already said, they suffer death for no cause whatsoever, their own headman gives them a mild chastisement. They marry once only in our manner, and only the eldest son marries, he is treated like the head of an entailed estate. The other brothers remain single all their lives. These Brahmenes keep their wives well guarded, and greatly honoured, so that no other man may sleep with them; if any of them die, they do not marry again, but if a woman wrongs her husband she is slain by poison. The brothers who remain bachelors sleep with the Nayar women, they hold it to be a great honour, and as they are Brahmenes no woman refuses herself to them, yet they may not sleep with any woman older than themselves. They dwell in their own houses and cities, and serve as clergy in the houses of worship, whither they go to pray at certain hours of the day, performing their rituals and idolatries.

Some of these Brahmenes serve the kings in every manner except in arms. No man may prepare any food for the King except a Brahmene or his own kin; they also serve as couriers to other countries with letters, money or merchandise, passing wherever they wish to go in safety and none does them any ill, even when the kings are at war. These Brahmenes are learned in their idolatry and possess many books thereof. The Kings hold them in high esteem.

I have already spoken many times of the Naiyars and yet I have not hitherto told you what manner of men they are. You are to know that in this land of Malabar there is another caste of people called Nayars and among them are noble men who have no other duty than to serve in war, and they always carry their arms withersoever they go, some swords and shields, others bows and arrows, and yet others spears. They all live with the King, and the other great Lords; nevertheless all receive stipends from the King or from the great Lords with whom they dwell. None may become a Nayar, save only he who is of Nayar lineage. They are very free from stain in their nobility. They will not touch anyone of low caste. Nor eat nor drink save in the house of a Nayar. These men are not married, their nephews (sister's sons) are their heirs. The Nayar women of good birth are very independent, and dispose of themselves as they please with Brahmenes and Nayars, but they do not sleep with men of caste lower than their own under pain of death. When they reach the age of twelve years their mothers hold a great ceremony. When a mother perceives that her daughter has attained that age, she asks her kinsfolk and friends to make ready to honour her daughter, then she asks of the kindred and especially of one particular kinsman or great friend to marry her daughter; this he willingly promises and then he has a small jewel made, which would contain a half ducat of gold, long like a ribbon, with a hole through the middle which comes out on the other side, strung on a thread of white silk. The mother then on a fixed day is present with her daughter gaily decked with many rich jewels, making great rejoicings with music and singing, and a great assembly of people. Then the kinsmen or friend comes bringing that jewel, and going through certain forms, throws it over the girl's neck. She wears it as a token all the rest of her life, and may then dispose of herself as she wills. The man departs without sleeping with her inasmuch as he is her kinsman; if he is not, he may sleep with her, but is not obliged to do so. Thenceforward the mother goes about searching and asking some young men to take her daughter's virginity; they must be Nayars and they regard it among themselves as a disgrace and a foul thing to take a woman's virginity. And when anyone has once slept with her, she is fit for association with men. Then the mother again goes about enquiring among other young Nayars if they wish to support her daughter, and take her as a Mistress so that three or four Nayars agree with her to keep her, and sleep with her, each paying her so much a day; the more lovers she has the greater is her honour. Each of one of them passes a day with her from midday on one day till midday on the next day and so they continue living quietly without any disturbance or quarrels among them. If any of them wishes to leave her, he leaves her, and takes another and she also if she is weary of a man, she tells him to go, and he does go, or makes terms with her. Any children they may have stay with the mother who has to bring them up, for they hold them not to be the children of any man, even if they bear his likeness, and they do not consider them their children, nor are they heirs to their estates, for as I have already stated their heirs are their nephews, sons of their sisters, (which rule whosoever will consider inwardly in his mind will find that it was established with a greater and deeper meaning than the common folk think) for they say that the Kings of the Nayars instituted it in order that the Nayars should not be held back from their service by the burden and labour of rearing children.

In this kingdom of Malabar there is also another caste of people whom they call Biabares, Indian Merchants, natives of the land. They deal in goods of every kind both in the seaports and inland, wheresoever their trade is of most profit. They gather to themselves all the pepper and ginger from the Nayars and husbandmen and ofttimes they buy the new crops beforehand in exchange for cotton clothes and other goods which they keep at the seaports. Afterwards they sell them again and gain much money thereby. Their privileges are such that the king of the country in which they dwell cannot execute them by legal process.

There is in this land yet another caste of folk known as Cuiavem. They do not differ from the Nayars, yet by reason of a fault which they committed, they remain separate from them. Their business is to make pottery and bricks for roofing the houses of the Kings and idols, which are roofed with bricks instead of tiles; only these, for as I have already said, other houses are thatched with branches. They have their own sort of idolatry, and their separate idols.

There is another Heathen caste which they call Mainatos, whose occupation is to wash clothes for the Kings, Brahmenes and Nayars. By this they live, and may not take up any other. There is another lower caste than these which they call Caletis, who are weavers who have no other way of earning save by weaving of cotton and silk clothes, but they are low caste folk and have but little money, so that they clothe the lower races. They are apart by themselves and have their own idolatry.

Besides the castes mentioned above, there are eleven others

lower than they with whom the others do not associate, nor do' they touch them under pain of death; and there are great distinctions between one and another of them, preserving them from mixture with one another. The purest of all these low, simple folk they call Tuias. Their work is mainly that of tending the palm-groves and gathering the fruit thereof, and carrying it away for wages on their backs, for there are no beasts of burden in the land.

There is another caste still lower than these whom they call Manen (Mancu in the printed text) who neither associate with others nor touch them, nor do the other touch them. They are washermen for the common people, and makers of sleeping mats from which occupations all but they are barred; their sons must perforce follow the same trade; they have their own separate idolatry.

There is another caste in this land still lower whom they call Canaquas. Their trade is making buckles and umbrellas. They learn letters for purposes of astronomy, they are great astrologers, and foretell with great truth things that are to come; there are some lords who maintain them for this cause.

There is also another lower caste, also Heathens, called Ageres. They are masons, carpenters, smiths, metal workers and some are goldsmiths, all of whom are of a common descent, and a separate caste, and have their idols apart from other folk. They marry, and their sons inherit their property, and learn their fathers' trade.

There is another caste still lower in this country called Mogeres, they are almost the same as the Tuias, but they do not touch one another. They work as carriers of all things belonging to the Royal State when it moves from one place to another, but there are very few of them in this land; they are a separate caste; they have no marriage law; the most of them gain their living on the sea, they are sailors, and some of them fishers; they have no Idols. They are as well slaves of the Nayars.

There is another caste yet lower whom they call Monquer, fishers who have no other work than fishing, yet some sail in the Moors' ship and in those of other Heathens, and they are very expert seamen. This race is very rude, they are shameless thieves; they marry and their sons succeed them, their women are of loose character, they sleep with anyone whosoever and it is held no evil. They have their own idolatry.

In this land of Malabar there is another caste of Heathen even lower than those, whom, they call Betunes. Their business is saltmaking and rice growing, they have no other livelihood.

They dwell in houses standing by themselves in the fields away from the roads, whither the gentlefolk do not walk. They have their own idolatry. They are slaves of the Kings and Nayars and pass their lives in poverty. The Nayars make them walk far away from them and speak to them from a far off. They hold no intercourse with any other caste.

There is another caste of Heathen, even lower and ruder, whom they call Paneens, who are great sorcerers and live by no other means.

There is another caste lower and ruder than they, named Revoleens a very poor folk, who live by carrying firewood and grass to the towns, they may touch none, nor may any touch them under pain of death. They go naked, covering only their private parts with scant and filthy rags, the more part of them indeed with leaves of certain trees. Their women wear many brass rings in their ears; and on their necks, arms and legs, necklaces and bracelets of heads.

And there is yet another caste of Heathens lower than these whom they call Poleas, who among all the rest are held to be accursed and excommunicate; they dwell in the fields and open campaigns in secret lurking places, whither folk of good caste never go save by mischance, and live in huts very strait and mean. They are tillers of rice with buffaloes and oxen. They never speak to the Nayars save from a far off, shouting so that they may hear them, and when they go along the roads they utter loud cries that they may be let past,

> and whosoever hears them leaves the road, and stands in the wood till they have passed by; and if anyone whether man or woman, touches them, his kinsfolk slay them forthwith, and in vengeance therefore they slay Poleas until they are weary without suffering any punishment.
>
> Yet another caste there is even lower and baser called Parens, who dwell in the most desert places away from all other castes. They have no intercourse with any person nor anyone with them; they are held to be worse than devils, and to be damned. Even to see them is to be unclean and outcaste. They eat yams and other roots of wild plants. They cover their middles with leaves, they also eat the flesh of wild beasts.
>
> With these end the distinctions between the castes of the Heathen, which are eighteen in all, each one separate and unable to touch others or marry with them; and besides these eighteen castes of the Heathen who are natives of Malabar, which I have now related to you, there are others of outlandish folk merchants and traders in the land, where they possess houses and estates, living like the natives yet with customs of their own.

These foreigners were not able to give a full and detailed picture of caste. This is understandable. For to every foreigner the private life of the Hindu is veiled and it is not possible for him to penetrate it. The social organism of India, the play of its motive forces, is moreover, regulated infinitely more by custom, carrying according to locality and baffling in its complexity, than by any legal formula which can be picked out of a legal textbook. But there is no doubt that caste did appear to the foreigner as the most singular and therefore the most distinguishing feature of Hindu society. Otherwise they would not have noted its existence in the record they made of what they observed when they came to India.

Caste therefore is something special in the Hindu social

organisation and marks off the Hindus from other peoples. Caste has been a growing institution. It has never been the same at all times. The shape and form of Caste as it existed when Megasthenes wrote his account was very different from what the shape and form it had taken when Alberuni came and the appearance it gave to the Portuguese was different from what it was in the time of Alberuni, But to understand caste one must have a more exact idea of its nature than these foreigners are able to give.

To follow the discussion of the subject of caste it is necessary to familiarize the reader with some basic conceptions which underlie the Hindu Social Organisation. The basic conception of social organisation which prevails among the Hindus starts with the rise of four classes or Varnas into which Hindu society is believed to have become divided. These four classes were named (1) Brahmans, the priestly and the educated class (2) Kshatriyas the military class (3) The Vaishyas the trading class and (4) The Shudras the servant class. For a time these were merely classes. After a time what were only classes (Varnas) became Castes (Jatis) and the four castes became four thousand. In this way the modern caste system was only the evolution of the ancient Varna system. No doubt the caste system is an evolution of the Varna system. But one can get no idea of the caste system by a study of the Varna system. Caste must be studied apart from Varna.

II

An old agnostic is said to have summed up his philosophy in the following word,

> 'The only thing I know is that I know nothing; and I am not quite sure that I know that'.

Sir Denzil Ibbetson[14] undertaking to write about caste in the Punjab said that the words of this agnostic about his philosophy expressed very exactly his own feelings regarding caste. It is no doubt true that owing to local circumstances there does appear a certain diversity about caste matters and that it is very difficult to make any statement regarding any one of the castes. Absolutely true as it may be, as regards one locality which will not be contradicted with equal truth as regards the same caste in some other area.

Although this may be true yet it cannot be difficult to separate the essential and fundamental features of caste from its non-essential and superficial features. An easy way to ascertain this is to ask what are the matters for which a person is liable to be excluded from caste. Mr. Bhattacharya[15] has stated the following as causes for expulsion from caste. (1) Embracing Christianity or Islam (2) Going to Europe or America (3) Marrying a widow (4) Publicly throwing the sacred thread (5) Publicly eating beef, pork or fowl (6) Publicly eating kachcha food prepared by a Mahomedan, Christian or low caste Hindu (7) Officiating at the house of a very low caste Shudra (8) By a female going away from home for immoral purposes (9) By a widow becoming pregnant. This list is not exhaustive and omits the three most important causes

[14] [*Editor's Note*: Sir Denzil Ibbetson of the Imperial Civil Service was one of the most important intellectual bureaucrats of the Census of India. As Deputy Superintendent for the Census of Punjab in 1881, Ibbetson pushed for a more ethnographic approach to data collection. His influence can be seen in the 1891 Census, which took occupational categories as far more central than Brahmanical ones.]

[15] [*Editor's Note*: Ambedkar most likely refers to Jogendranath Bhattacharya, who is the author of *Hindu Castes and Sects: An Exposition of the Origin of the Hindu Caste System and the Bearing of the Sects toward Each Other and toward Other Religious Systems*, Calcutta: Thacker Spink, 1896. As the head of the Bengal Brahman Sabha, Bhattacharya defended caste as the essence of Hindu society. In *Hindu Castes and Sects*, Bhattacharya wrote, that while caste is an 'iron chain' for lower castes, for the 'higher classes caste is a golden chain which they have willingly placed around their neck, and which has fixed them to only that which is noble and praiseworthy'.]

which entail expulsion from caste. They are (10) Intermarrying outside caste (11) Interdining with persons of another caste and (12) Change of occupation. The second defect in the statement of Mr. Bhattacharya is that it does not make any distinction between essentials and non-essentials.

Of course, when a person is expelled from his caste the penalty is uniform. His friends, relatives and fellowmen refuse to partake of his hospitality. He is not invited to entertainments in their houses. He cannot obtain brides or bridegrooms for his children. Even his married daughters cannot visit him without running the risk of being excluded from caste. His priest, his barber and washerman refuse to serve him. His fellow castemen sever their connection with him so completely that they refuse to assist him even at the funeral of a member of his household. In some cases the man excluded from caste is debarred access to public temples and to the cremation or burial ground. These reasons for expulsion from caste indirectly show the rules and regulations of the caste. But all regulations are not fundamental. There are many which are unessential. Caste can exist even without them. The essential and unessential can be distinguished by asking another question. When can a Hindu who has lost caste regain his caste? The Hindus have a system of Prayaschitas which are Penances and which a man who has been expelled from caste must perform before he can be admitted to caste fellowship. With regard to these Prayaschitas or Penances certain points must be remembered. In the first place, there are caste offences for which there is no Prayaschita. In the second place, the Prayaschitas vary according to the offence. In some cases the Prayaschitas involve a very small penalty. In other cases the penalty involved is a very severe one.

The existence of a Prayaschita and the absence of it have a significance which must be clearly understood. The absence of Prayaschita does not mean that anyone may commit the offence with impunity. On the contrary it means that the offence is of an immeasurable magnitude and the offender once expelled is beyond reclamation. There is no reentry for him in the caste from which he is expelled. The existence of a Prayaschita means that the offence is compoundable. The offender can take the prescribed Prayaschita and obtain admission in the caste from which he is expelled.

There are two offences for which there is no penance. These are (1) change from Hindu Religion to another religion (2) Marriage with a person of another caste or another religion. It is obvious if a man loses caste for these offences he loses it permanently. Of the other offences the Prayaschitas prescribed are of the severest kind, are two – (1) interdining with a person of another caste or a non-Hindu and (2) Taking to occupation which is not the occupation of the caste. In the case of the other offences the penalty is a light one almost nominal.

The surest clue to find out what are the fundamental rules of caste and what caste consists it is furnished by the rules regarding Prayaschitas. Those for the infringement of which there is no Prayaschita constitute the very soul of caste and those for the infringement of which the Prayaschita is of the severest kind make up the body of caste. It may therefore be said without any hesitation that there are four fundamental rules of caste. A caste may be defined as a social group having (a) belief in Hindu Religion and bound by certain regulations as to (b) marriage (c) food and (d) occupation. To this one more characteristic may be added namely a social group having a common name by which it is recognised.

In the matter of marriage the regulation lays down that the caste must be endogamous. There can be no intermarriage between members of different castes. This is the first and the most fundamental idea on which the whole fabric of the caste is built up.

In the matter of food the rule, is that a person cannot take food from and dine with any person who does not belong to his caste. This means that only those who can intermarry can also interdine. Those who cannot intermarry cannot interdine. In other words, caste is an endogamous unit and also a communal unit.

In the matter of occupation the regulation is that a person must follow the occupation which is the traditional occupation of his caste and if the caste has no occupation then he should follow the occupation of his father.

In the matter of status of a person it is fixed and is hereditary. It is fixed because a person's status is determined by the status of the caste to which he belongs. It is hereditary because a Hindu is stamped with the caste to which his parents belonged, a Hindu cannot change his status because he cannot change his caste. A Hindu is born in a caste and he dies a member of the caste in which he is born. A Hindu may lose his status if he loses caste. But he cannot acquire a new or a better or different status.

What is the significance of a common name for a caste? The significance of this will be clear if we ask two questions which are very relevant and a correct answer to each is necessary for a complete idea of this institution of caste. Social groups are either organized or unorganized. When the membership of the group and the process of joining and leaving the groups, are the subject of definite social regulations and involve certain duties and privileges in relation to other members of the group then the group is an organized group. A group is a voluntary group in which members enter with a full knowledge of what they are doing and the aims which the association is designed to fulfill. On the other hand, there are groups of which an individual person becomes a member without any act of volition, and becomes subject to social regulation and traditions over which he has no control of any kind.

Now it is hardly necessary to say that caste is a highly organized social grouping. It is not a loose or a floating body. Similarly, it is not necessary to say that caste is an involuntary grouping. A Hindu is born in a caste and he dies as a member of that caste. There is no Hindu without caste, cannot escape caste and being bounded by caste from birth to death he becomes subject to social regulations and traditions of the caste over which he has no control.

The significance of a separate name for a caste lies in this – namely it makes caste an organized and an involuntary grouping. A separate and a distinctive name for a caste makes caste asking to a corporation with a perpetual existence and a seal of separate entity. The significance of separate names for separate castes has not been sufficiently realised by writers on caste. In doing that they have lost sight of a most distinctive feature of caste. Social groups there are and they are bound to be in every society. Many social groups in many countries can be equated to various castes in India and may be regarded as their equivalent. Potters, Washermen, Intellectuals as social groups are everywhere. But in other countries they have remained as unorganised and voluntary groups while in India they have become organised and involuntary i.e., they have become castes because in other countries the social groups were not given name while in India they did. It is the name which the caste bears which gives it fixity and continuity and individuality. It is the name which defines who are its members and in most cases a person born in a caste carries the name of the caste as a part of his surname. Again it is the name which makes it easy for the caste to enforce its rules and regulations. It makes it easy in two ways. In the first place, the name of the caste forming a surname of the individual prevents the offender in passing off as a person belonging to another caste and thus escape the jurisdiction of the caste. Secondly, it helps to identify the offending individual and the caste to whose jurisdiction he is subject so that he is easily handed up and punished for any breach of the caste rules.

This is what caste means. Now as to the caste system. This

involves the study of the mutual relations between different castes. Looked at as a collection of caste, the caste system presents several features which at once strike the observer. In the first place there is no inter-connection between the various castes which form a system. Each caste is separate and distinct. It is independent and sovereign in the disposal of its internal affairs and the enforcement of caste regulations. The castes touch but they do not interpenetrate. The second feature relates to the order in which one caste stands in relation to the other castes in the system. That order is vertical and not horizontal.

Such is the caste and such is the caste system. Question is, is this enough to know the Hindu social organisation? For a static conception of the Hindu social organisation an idea of the caste and the caste system is enough. One need not trouble to remember more than the facts that the Hindus are divided into castes and that the castes form a system in which all hang on a thread which runs through the system in such a way that while encircling and separating one caste from another it holds them all as though it was a string of tennis balls hanging one above the other. But this will not be enough to understand caste as a dynamic phenomenon. To follow the workings of caste in action it is necessary to note one other feature of caste besides the caste system, namely class-caste system.

The relationship between the ideas of caste and class has been a matter of lively controversy. Some say that caste is analogous to class and that there is no difference between the two. Others hold that the idea of castes is fundamentally opposed to that of class. This is an aspect of the subject of caste about which more will be said hereafter. For the present it is necessary to emphasize one feature of the caste system which has not been referred to hereinbefore. It is this. Although caste is different from and opposed to the notion of class yet the caste system – as distinguished from caste

– recognizes a class system which is somewhat different from the graded status referred to above. Just as the Hindus are divided into so many castes, castes are divided into different classes of castes. The Hindu is caste-conscious. He is also class conscious. Whether he is caste conscious or class conscious depends upon the caste with which he comes in conflict. If the caste with which he comes in conflict is a caste within the class to which he belongs he is caste conscious. If the caste is outside the class to which he belongs he is class conscious. Anyone who needs any evidence on this point may study the Non-Brahman Movement in the Madras and the Bombay Presidency. Such a study will leave no doubt that to a Hindu caste periphery is as real as class periphery and caste consciousness is as real as class consciousness.

Caste, it is said, is an evolution of the Varna system. I will show later on that this is nonsense. Caste is a perversion of Varna. At any rate it is an evolution in the opposite direction. But while caste has completely perverted the Varna system it has borrowed the class system from the Varna system. Indeed the class-caste system follows closely the class cleavages of the Varna system.

Looking at the caste system from this point of view one comes across several lives of class cleavage which run through this pyramid of castes dividing the pyramid into blocks of castes. The first line of cleavage follows the line of division noticeable in the ancient Chaturvarna system. The old system of Chaturvarna made a distinction between the first three Varnas, the Brahmans, Kshatriyas, Vaishyas and the fourth Varna namely the Shudra. The three former were classes as the Regenerate classes. The Shudra was held as the Unregenerate class. This distinction was based upon the fact that the former were entitled to wear the sacred thread and study the Vedas. The Shudra was entitled to neither and that is why he was regarded as the unregenerate class. This line of cleavage is still in existence and forms the basis of the present day class division separating the castes which have grown out of the vast class of Shudras from those which have grown out of the three classes of Brahmans, the Kshatriyas and Vaishyas. This line of class cleavage is the one which is expressed by the terms High Castes and Low Castes and which are short forms for the High Class Castes and Low Class Castes.

Next after this line of cleavage there runs through the pyramid a second line of class cleavage. It runs just below the Low Class Castes. It sets above all the castes born out of the four Varnas i.e., the High Castes as well as the low castes above the remaining castes which 1 will merely describe as the 'rest'. This line of class cleavage is again a real one and follows the well-defined distinction which was a fundamental principle of the Chaturvarna system. The Chaturvarna system as is pointed out made a distinction between the four Varnas putting the three Varnas above the fourth. But it also made an equally clear distinction between those within the Chaturvarna and those outside the Chaturvarna. It had a terminology to express this distinction. Those within the Chaturvarna – high or low, Brahman or Shudra were called Savarna i. e., those with the stamp of the Varna. Those outside the Chaturvarna were called Avarna i. e., those without the stamp of Varna. All the castes which have evolved out of the four varnas are called Savarna Hindus – which is rendered in English by the term Caste Hindus – The 'rest' are the Avarnas who in present parlance spoken of by Europeans as Non-caste Hindus i.e., those who are outside the four original castes or varnas.

Much that is written about the caste system has reference mostly to the caste system among the Savarna Hindus. Very little is known about the Avarna Hindus. Who are these Avarna Hindus, what is their position in Hindu Society, how are they related to the Savarna Hindus are questions to which no attention has so far been paid. I am sure that without considering these questions no one can get a true picture of the social structure the Hindus have built. To leave out the Class cleavage between the Savarna Hindus and the Avarna Hindus is to relate Grimm's Fairy Tale which leaves out the witches, the goblins and the ogres. The Avarna Hindus comprise three . . .

[Manuscript breaks off.]

Born into an 'untouchable' family, BHIMRAO RAMJI AMBEDKAR (1891-1956) was one of India's most radical thinkers. A brilliant student, he earned doctorates in economics from both Columbia University, New York, and the London School of Economics. In 1936, the year he wrote *Annihilation of Caste*, Ambedkar founded the Independent Labour Party. The ILP contested the 1937 Bombay election to the Central Legislative Assembly for the 13 reserved and 4 general seats, and secured 11 and 3 seats respectively. He was India's first Minister for Law and Justice, and oversaw the drafting of the Indian Constitution. Ambedkar eventually embraced Buddhism, a few months before his death in 1956. Ambedkar's abiding interest in the communist movement and Marxism is evident from the beginning of his public life to his last days when he delivered a speech comparing Karl Marx with Buddha.

ANAND TELTUMBDE is a civil rights activist, political analyst, columnist and author of many books. He has had a long association with peoples' struggles, spanning over three decades. Trained in technology and management he marshals his insights of the modern techno-managerial world to sharpen strategies of struggles. His recent books are *Mahad: The Making of the First Dalit Revolt* (Aakar, 2016), *Dalits: Past, Present and Future* (Routledge, 2016), *Persistence of Castes* (Zed Books, 2006), *Anti-Imperialism and Annihilation of Castes* (Ramai, 2004). He writes a column 'Margin Speak' in *Economic & Political Weekly*.